The Seeds of Suspicion
Are Planted . . .

Madeline gulped. "Dr. McDuff said he is sure that Colin Bickley died from some kind of poisoning."

"How dreadful. How the poor man must have suffered." Cecily still couldn't understand why Madeline should be so upset by the news—until she spoke again, and then it all became abundantly clear.

"Dr. McDuff thought the poison was cyanide at first, because Colin's skin had a blue tinge to it. But there was no smell of bitter almonds, which ruled it out. Upon further examination, Dr. McDuff decided some kind of poisonous plant killed Colin." She stopped wringing her hands and clasped Cecily's arm. Her fingers felt deathly cold.

"Cecily," Madeline said in a low, urgent voice, "Colin Bickley was at my house last night. I cooked him a meal, which he ate. A few hours later he was dead."

MORE MYSTERIES FROM
THE BERKLEY PUBLISHING GROUP . . .

DO NOT DISTURB

KATE KINGSBURY

JOVE BOOKS, NEW YORK

DO NOT DISTURB

A Jove Book / published by arrangement with
the author

PRINTING HISTORY
Jove edition / January 1994

ISBN: 0-515-11282-8

A JOVE BOOK®
Jove Books are published by The Berkley Publishing Group,
200 Madison Avenue, New York, New York 10016.
JOVE and the "J" design are trademarks belonging
to Jove Publications, Inc.

PRINTED IN THE UNITED STATES OF AMERICA

10 9 8 7 6 5 4 3 2 1

CHAPTER

❖ 1 ❖

The summer of 1906 had been cool and damp in England. Nevertheless, autumn came slowly to the village of Badgers End and its sheltered cove on the southeast coast.

The season began with a crisp, clean chill in the breeze from the English Channel and a tinge of gold to the willow leaves that hung over Deep Willow Pond. Acrid smoke curled from chimney pots and drifted lazily across Putney Downs, and the sun threw long shadows a little earlier each day.

Hawthorne Lane crossed the Downs in a meandering trail of hedgerows and wildflowers, barely leaving room for the cart horses pulling their loads to market. Usually the lane became deserted by sundown, except for the stray rabbit or inquisitive hedgehog.

This evening, however, as dusk seeped over the countryside, four grubby-faced urchins dressed in shabby knicker-bockers stole along the lane, one behind the other.

A muffled giggle disturbed the quiet peace, and the leader of the group twisted his head with an urgent "Sshhh!"

"Shut up, you blithering idiots," someone else whispered, and the laughter was suppressed.

The straggly line continued in silence, except for the occasional scrape of a boot against the surface of the road. Soon the boys reached the cliffs and could look down from their lofty perch to the dark blue cove below with its crescent of golden sand. Ahead of them stood a row of cottages.

Hidden by the tall hedges that lined the lane, they conferred with hand signals. Then one by one they each crept silently up to a front door. Quickly each boy tied one end of thick cotton thread to the door knocker, then scuttled back to the shelter of the hedges.

The leader of the group, a tough-looking redhead with protruding ears, lifted his hand. Four fists clutched four lengths of thread, trembling with anticipation.

The signaling hand fell, and four fists jerked at once. The door knockers clattered in a cacophony of sound, setting off a furious chorus of barking dogs.

Three of the doors opened as if on cue, one after the other. After a short pause, two men and a woman stepped outside, looking across at each other in bewilderment.

With a loud snort of uncontrolled laughter, one of the boys raced down the lane, followed by his three compan-ions, all with fists shoved in their mouths to curb the sound of their glee.

Looking after them, the woman said sharply, "Those boys and that stupid game. Ought to know better, they did." Her neighbors shook their heads and, amid muttered curses, returned to their fireplaces. Peace settled once more over Hawthorne Lane.

The sun gradually sank out of sight, abandoning the sky to the moon. The shadows merged, softened, and reap-peared, bathed in a ghostly pale light.

A man walked steadily along the lane, from the direction of the cove. In spite of the steep climb, his breathing sounded even in the shrouded silence of the Downs.

The cottages were in darkness, the inhabitants having succumbed to the weariness of long hours in the fields. The man strode past them all, his firm footsteps echoing behind him. Reaching the last cottage in the row, he opened the door with a key and disappeared inside.

Sometime later, a single rap of a door knocker once more disturbed the peace in the lane. This time the summons had been served on the door of the end cottage.

The man inside cursed. He was just about to snuggle down in his bed, his hot-water bottle already warming the sheets. He was inclined to ignore the knock, in the hopes that whoever it was would go away.

But he couldn't. There was always the possibility that it could be someone from the work site, some problem that needed his immediate attention.

Muttering to himself, the man turned up the wick of the oil lamp. In the flickering light, he shuffled down the passageway to the door and dragged it open.

Frowning, he leaned forward, peering into the darkness. He could see no one out there. Surely he hadn't imagined the knock? He thought he heard a slight sound, a soft movement in the shadows. He stepped outside for a better look. Still he could see nothing but the outline of the hedges against the dark sky.

The damp night air chilled his bones, and he turned impatiently back to the warmth of the cottage. Something touched his neck, and he lifted a hand to explore. He took a couple of steps, then blinked. His eyelids felt curiously heavy. He hadn't realized how desperately tired he felt—so tired he couldn't lift his eyelids again.

He couldn't open his eyes. He felt odd; his face seemed stiff, his jaw tight. He tried to grimace, but his mouth wouldn't move. His chin dropped, and try as he might he couldn't lift his head.

Panic rose, swift and terrifying, as he staggered, one hand

groping for the door frame. He couldn't swallow. His lungs felt as though they were gripped in a steel vise, tightening, tightening . . .

The pain was terrible. His legs buckled, writhing in agony, while the top half of him seemed frozen solid. He couldn't breathe . . . the awful agony of it . . . he twitched violently . . . then lay still.

By midmorning Cecily Sinclair had finished her rounds of the gardens and sat relaxing in the library of the Pennyfoot Hotel, awaiting the arrival of Phoebe Carter-Holmes and Madeline Pengrath, the members of her entertainment committee.

Although the waning of the season meant a lull in the social activities at the hotel, Cecily still liked to arrange something for the few guests who chose to visit the tiny seaside town during the quieter months.

The cool, mellow autumn days always brought a special feeling of pleasurable relief after the hectic weeks of summer. The Pennyfoot had gained a considerable reputation as a unique and elegant retreat for the jaded upper class of the big city.

From May to September its rooms were filled, enjoyed by the elite in their pursuit of pleasure, safe in the knowledge that their indiscretions would be kept secret by the remarkably discreet staff of the hotel.

James Sinclair, Cecily's late husband, had chosen his employees with the utmost care, leaving each of them in no doubt of their fate should they ever breathe one word of the goings-on behind the Pennyfoot's sedate white walls.

It was a measure of the staff's loyalty that no word of scandal had ever touched the name of the Pennyfoot Hotel. Cecily was very proud of that. And now that her beloved James was gone, taken by the malaria he'd contracted while serving in Her Majesty's Service in the tropics, Cecily was more determined than ever that his legacy be maintained in the manner he had dictated.

That was the main reason Cecily had taken over some of

the duties as owner of the hotel. The renovations James had undertaken still left heavy debts, and Cecily was determined to keep the hotel in the family, as James had requested at his death.

Seated at the head of the long mahogany table, Cecily glanced up at her husband's portrait hanging over the huge marble fireplace. At forty-three she was much too young to be a widow, she thought sadly. Who would have imagined, when James first acquired what had once been the family home of the Earl of Saltchester, that a few short years later he would die, much too soon, leaving her to carry on alone?

The paneled door opened, cutting short her reverie. A very large hat appeared, loaded down with ostrich feathers, with a swathe of cream chiffon enveloping huge bronze and dark red chrysanthemums. The middle-aged face underneath it smiled, while a pair of bright blue eyes gazed across the room.

"Cecily, dear, am I late? I'm so sorry. Algie was fussing over his sermon for Sunday and insisted I listen to it. Sometimes I wonder what he'd do if I weren't around to hold his hand. There can't be many vicars who have a mother willing to spend so much time helping them with their work."

Cecily smiled back. "Come in, Phoebe. No, you're not late. I came in early. It's getting a little cool to stay out in the gardens too long in the mornings. The sea breeze can be very fresh."

The hat nodded vigorously, threatening to overbalance had it not been securely pinned. "I know exactly what you mean. I shall have to dig out my winter coats and muffs before the east wind gets a bite to it."

The door opened again, and a willowy woman dressed in pale mauve muslin swept in. Long dark hair flowed free and settled about her shoulders, and her expressive dark eyes flitted about the room, never still.

"My goodness," she murmured in a low, whispery voice that always reminded Cecily of windblown rushes, "I do declare, the evil spirits are about in force today. I can feel them all around me."

"Oh, for heaven's sake, Madeline, please don't start that again," Phoebe complained, carefully smoothing her green silk skirt as she sat on the padded chair behind the table.

Madeline paused long enough to give Phoebe a disdainful sniff before floating over to a chair on the opposite side of the table, in front of the massive bookshelves. Shaking her hair back from her face with a toss of her head, she looked at Cecily. "At least you have the good sense to take heed of what I say."

Cecily shifted uncomfortably on her chair. It was true that Madeline had an uncanny knack for sensing trouble. In fact, Madeline had a certain strange aptitude for all kinds of things.

Her talent for healing various ailments with potions concocted from plants grown in her abundant garden caused much speculation among the villagers. Half of them swore that Madeline's potions worked far better than anything the doctor could prescribe, while the other half were convinced that they'd be possessed by demons if they so much as touched a leaf from one of her plants.

The fact of the matter was, Madeline had earned the dubious reputation of being, at best, a gypsy changeling and, at worst, a witch. The woman's appearance went a long way toward fostering that belief.

Although Cecily was quite sure that Madeline was close to her own age, the woman's gleaming black hair revealed not a single strand of gray, and her skin was as smooth and soft as a young woman of twenty.

Compared to Madeline, Cecily felt positively ancient, what with her sensible light brown chignon sprinkled with silver and the deep laughter lines at the corners of her eyes.

"Well," Phoebe said, opening her handbag to pull out a lace-edged handkerchief, "I'm quite sure your evil spirits are nothing more than those little hooligans running around playing that Knock Down Ginger. Such an annoying game.

I'm so tired of answering my door to thin air, and Algie swears his nerves have been shattered by the little devils."

"Algie's nerves can be shattered by a sneeze," Madeline said dryly.

Sensing the usual confrontation between the two women, Cecily launched into a discussion of the tea dance planned for that week.

Madeline, who took care of all the floral arrangements, outlined her ideas, and Phoebe, as entertainments director, described the women's violin quartet she'd hired. The details had just been finalized when a smart tap sounded on the door. All three heads turned toward the sound as Cecily called out, "Yes, come in."

The tall, broad-shouldered man who entered wore a worried frown on his pleasant features. "Please excuse the intrusion, madam, but I thought you should know right away. We have a small problem in the bathrooms."

Cecily regarded her manager with anxious eyes. Baxter never consulted her unless the matter was serious. "What kind of problem?" she asked warily.

"I'm afraid it is a plumbing problem, madam. We shall have to close the bathrooms down until it is taken care of. I have sent for the plumber, but he is in Wellercombe at the moment, and it could be some time before he arrives. I felt that you should be informed."

Cecily raised her eyebrows. "All three bathrooms?"

"All three." Baxter lifted his hands in a helpless gesture. "I'm sorry, madam."

"Yes, well, I'm sure it's not your fault. Thank you, Baxter."

Instead of leaving, Baxter remained where he was, an odd expression on his face.

Cecily frowned. "Was there something else?"

"I wasn't sure if you'd heard, madam. About the foreman of the lighthouse project?"

Madeline sat up straight as Cecily continued to gaze at her manager. "What about the foreman, Baxter?"

"He's dead, madam. They found him lying outside his

cottage this morning. Apparently he died of a heart attack."

Since Cecily didn't know the man in question personally, Baxter's news wasn't all that startling. What was startling was Madeline's reaction to it. With a strangled cry she leapt to her feet, one hand clutching her throat. Then, without a word she fled from the room, leaving the rest of the occupants staring after her in surprise.

"Well!" Phoebe exclaimed, fluttering her handkerchief in front of her face. "Whatever is the matter with her, I do wonder?"

Cecily privately wondered the same thing, though all she said was, "You know how sensitive Madeline is. She is devastated if she finds a dead bird."

"A dead bird, yes." Phoebe sniffed. "However, I have yet to see Madeline display such lavish emotion over a human being. Until now, that is." Luckily the more macabre details of Baxter's announcement held more interest for her, and she added, "Will he be buried here, do you think? It has been a while since Algie had a funeral. I do so enjoy funerals."

Baxter raised his eyebrows. Catching Cecily's gaze, he rolled his eyes to the ceiling in an expression of disbelief.

Phoebe, who had her back to him, gushed on. "Not that I like to see people die, of course, but once they are dead, I mean, there's not much you can do about it, can you? You might as well enjoy the send-off, as I'm sure they would also, if—"

"Mrs. Carter-Holmes," Baxter interrupted, in a rare display of impropriety, "I do believe Mrs. Chubb was looking for you. I told her I would inform you at the earliest opportunity."

For a moment Phoebe looked affronted at this rude intrusion into her conversation, but then curiosity got the better of her. "Did she say what she wanted?" she asked, getting up from her chair with a rustle of silk.

"I'm afraid not."

"Ah, well, then, I had better go and find out for myself. Thank you, Mr. Baxter." She reached the door and looked back. "Oh, Cecily, I very nearly forgot. I would like to discuss the church bazaar with you, if you have time this afternoon? Perhaps you could meet me in Dolly's Tea Shop? About three o'clock?"

Cecily smiled. "Of course, Phoebe. I'd be happy to meet you."

"Fine. Then I will see you later."

The door closed behind her, barely preceding Baxter's exasperated grunt. "That woman," he muttered darkly, "has the sensitivity of a wild boar."

In spite of herself, Cecily had to laugh. "She means well. She doesn't always think before she speaks, but her heart is in the right place."

He made a sound of disgust. "I do not understand how she could prattle on like that. Surely she hasn't forgotten whose funeral was the last one to be held at St. Bartholomew's?"

Touched by his concern, she said gently, "It's all right, Baxter. It has been almost ten months, after all."

"If I might be permitted to point out, madam, that is not a long time for the pain to fade. To be reminded so irreverently of your loss must be most distressing."

"James would not want me to be miserable on his behalf for too long." She glanced down at her hands to hide the sudden surge of emotion that could still catch her unawares. "I'm quite sure Phoebe would be horrified if she thought she had caused me any anguish."

"Perhaps. However, I do wish the woman would watch her tongue."

"Oh, come now, Baxter. Life would be very dull without friends like Phoebe. She can be most entertaining at times."

Baxter looked down his nose. "So I assume. Mr. Rawlins seems quite taken with her, though I can't imagine why."

Cecily looked at him in astonishment. "Mr. Rawlins? I wasn't aware that he'd met Phoebe." A mental picture formed in her mind of the short, frail figure of the artist who had booked into the hotel the day before. With his flowing locks, huge dark eyes, and pallid complexion, he reminded her of the statue of Jesus hanging above the altar in St. Bartholomew's.

"Mr. Rawlins caught sight of Mrs. Carter-Holmes this morning and inquired as to her name. When I informed him, he seemed quite disappointed, until I mentioned the fact that she was a widow. At that he brightened considerably. He asked me to introduce him at the first opportunity."

"Really," Cecily murmured. "How intriguing. They are around the same age, of course. But I wouldn't have thought . . ." She let the sentence trail off. She knew only too well what it was like to be lonely.

"Madam?"

She looked up to see a hint of concern in Baxter's light gray eyes. She smiled. "No matter. I hope you will engineer an introduction as soon as possible. It will do Phoebe a world of good."

Baxter's expression portrayed his extreme doubts, but he refrained from answering.

Cecily decided it was time to change the subject. "Now, tell me more about this poor man who died," she demanded.

"I'm afraid I know very little about it. The postman told me the news. He was up at Hawthorne Cottages when they took the poor devil away. Only a young chap, so the postman said. Couldn't have been thirty."

"Oh, how awful. His poor family." Cecily glanced up at James's portrait. She knew how it was to lose a beloved one before his time. She'd expected him to go on living forever. Certainly into old age, in any case.

"I wonder if Madeline knew the foreman," she added, remembering the woman's sudden dash from the room. "She seemed very upset at the news."

"I assume that she had some acquaintance with him," Baxter said delicately.

Cecily sighed. They both knew quite well Madeline's reputation for befriending strangers. Most of the rumors, Cecily felt sure, were misconstrued. Of course, Madeline's private life was her own concern and nobody else's, but Cecily couldn't help wishing her friend were a little more prudent in her choice of companionship. Something told her that this time Madeline could have made a serious mistake.

CHAPTER

❖ 2 ❖

"You will let me know when the plumber has solved the problem with the bathrooms?" Cecily said as Baxter made a move to leave.

"Of course, madam. I trust it won't be too long before he gets here."

"I certainly hope not. We'll have some very disgruntled guests as it is."

"There is the outdoor privy if anyone is desperate."

Cecily pulled a face. "Well, I suppose that will have to do. Just the thought of people having to go outdoors makes me ill. How quickly one gets used to modern conveniences. I had no such concern when I was growing up, however."

"We are spoiled indeed, madam."

He avoided her gaze, staring over her head when she answered, "Oh, come now, Baxter. I'm well aware of your distrust of change, but even you have to admit that modern plumbing is a vast improvement over the outdoor privy. Why, the smell alone is enough to kill a person. Can you imagine the diseases that must lurk in that dreadful hut?"

"It served very well for centuries," Baxter said stubbornly.

Cecily shook her head in mock despair. She rarely won that particular argument with her manager. Changing the subject again, she leaned forward and lowered her voice to a conspiratorial whisper.

"Baxter, do you by any chance have one of those little cigars with you?"

His eyelids flickered, but his expression remained inscrutable. "Yes, madam."

"May I please have one?"

He dropped his disapproving gaze to her face. "As I have mentioned on several occasions, I do not wish to encourage you in such a despicable habit, madam."

She smiled sweetly. "Despicable for whom, Baxter?"

Apparently realizing the pit she led him toward, he struggled with his answer for a moment, then said a little desperately, "I have made my opinion clear on that subject many times."

"You have indeed, Baxter," Cecily said, beginning to enjoy herself. "What is acceptable and pleasurable for men is a despicable habit for women. Isn't that what you are trying to tell me?"

He gave up the contest far too quickly. Digging into the pocket of his waistcoat, he withdrew the familiar slim packet and handed it to her.

"Thank you, Baxter." She extracted a thin cigar from the pack and handed him back the remaining one. "Now if you'd be so kind as to light it for me?"

He lifted his chin and stretched his neck against the stiff white collar he wore. Aggravating her with his slow movements, he patted the pocket of his black morning coat before drawing out the box of matches.

Cecily waited impatiently while he struck the match, then

finally leaned forward to light the cigar. "Thank you," she said, exhaling a cloud of smoke.

Baxter's mouth tightened. He dropped the matches into his pocket. "If you will excuse me, madam, I must return to my duties."

"Of course." Cecily waved the cigar at him. "Would you please arrange for a trap to take me into town at half past two this afternoon?"

"Yes, madam." He glanced up at James's portrait with an expression of resignation, then disappeared through the door.

Cecily smiled. James had extracted one promise from Baxter as he lay dying. He had asked his manager and good friend to take care of his wife after he had departed from this good earth. Baxter was inclined to take that request far too seriously at times.

She blew smoke at the portrait and murmured out loud, "I'm sorry, James. I know you wouldn't approve, and had you not left me, I might never have started this habit. But the world is changing, my love, and I must change with it."

Sighing, she stubbed out the cigar in the silver ashtray and pushed back her chair.

Altheda Chubb took an enormous amount of pride in her job. As head housekeeper of the Pennyfoot, she could enjoy what she did best—creating order out of chaos. Give her a dirty, untidy house, and she could have it spanking neat and clean in a matter of hours.

The Pennyfoot presented a challenge, and Altheda rose magnificently to the occasion. A chubby, good-natured woman, she nevertheless ruled her little domain with an iron hand. She was the general and the maids her troops, and between them they kept the reputation of the hotel untarnished and as spotless as the polished floors and sparkling windows.

Therefore, when she whisked through the dining room on her morning tour of inspection and found the white tablecloths bare of any utensils, let alone the china place settings, she tackled the problem with her usual gusto.

Mrs. Chubb billowed into the spacious kitchen with her arms folded across her bountiful breasts and glared at the housemaid standing by the window. "Gertie, for heaven's sake look sharp, will you? I don't know what's the matter with you, I'm sure I don't."

Gertie turned dark, soulful eyes in the housekeeper's direction. "I didn't get much sleep last night. I'm bloody tired." She stomped over to the dresser, the hem of her long black skirt stirring up a small cloud of flour that had been spilled on the stone floor.

Heading for the broom cupboard, Mrs. Chubb declared, "I'll make you tired, my girl, if you don't get out there this minute. Breakfast will be served in the dining room in less than an hour, and all the tables still have to be laid. This is Ethel's day off, and you know it will take you twice as long on your own."

"I'm going," Gertie muttered, tucking back a stray black curl where it belonged under her cap. "Anyway, I don't know what all the bleeding fuss is about. The hotel's half-empty, ain't it? It's the end of season now. We ain't going to see a full crowd again till Christmas."

"We still have to lay all the tables, as well you know, and madam will be down to breakfast now that the hotel's quiet. Besides, we had two new guests book in yesterday. We want to make a good impression on them, don't we?"

"Yeah, I saw one of them. Looked like a bleeding witch, she did, what with that thick black veil hiding her face." Gertie looked thoughtful. "Maybe she is a witch, come to think of it. She's blinking strange, if you ask me."

In spite of herself, Mrs. Chubb surrendered to her curiosity. "What do you mean, 'strange'?"

Gertie settled her back against the dresser. "Well, she's such a big bugger for a woman. Not fat, mind, but . . . big. And have you seen the size of her clodhoppers? They're bloody huge." She spread out her hands, palms facing each other.

Mrs. Chubb shrugged. "Lots of women have big feet."

Gertie gave her a broad wink. "Yeah, but do lots of 'em clomp around like a bleeding navvy? I can just see her humping a sack of coal on them shoulders."

Deciding that she'd given Gertie enough leeway for one day, Mrs. Chubb said crisply, "I understand that Mrs. Parmentier has recently lost her husband. You'd clomp around, too, if you'd just become a widow. Anyway, that's enough of that talk. You know madam doesn't like gossip, and I do wish you'd watch that tongue of yours. That kind of language is most unbecoming for a young lady."

"I never saw madam clomp around when she was widowed," Gertie said stubbornly. "I tell you that woman is bloody strange."

Giving up on her frequently useless attempts to clean up Gertie's speech, Mrs. Chubb clapped her hands together. "All right, my girl. Get to it if you want to keep your job."

Considering the housemaid towered over her by several inches, she had difficulty asserting her authority effectively.

Gertie muttered something about not caring, and Mrs. Chubb peered more closely at the housemaid's face. Now that she thought about it, the girl did look poorly. And Gertie didn't usually complain about her job. She had always loved working at the Pennyfoot Hotel.

"Is something worrying you?" Mrs. Chubb asked, quite anxious now. What with all the eligible girls leaving for London to go into service with the upper crust, housemaids were hard to come by. And Gertie had been at the Pennyfoot for five years now, since she was twelve years old.

Actually Gertie had done things back to front and left London to work at the seaside, which made her all the more unusual. Although the housekeeper would never admit it to her face, Gertie was a good, reliable worker, and in spite of an abysmal lack of control over her tongue, the Pennyfoot would not be the same without her.

Gertie's shoulders rose and fell, dislodging a strap of her apron. "It's Ian," she said mournfully. "He's left."

"Left town?"

Gertie shook her head, and her cap slipped sideways. Pinning it back in place, she said, "Nah. Left the Pennyfoot. Said he didn't want to be a footman no more. He's gone to work on that new lighthouse they're building on Doom Point."

Mrs. Chubb relaxed. "Ah, well, you'll still see him, then, won't you? It's not like he's gone back to London or anything."

"Not the bleeding same, though, is it?" Gertie said, opening the drawer containing the silverware. She dragged out a tray loaded with utensils, then nudged the drawer shut with a solid hip.

Scowling at Mrs. Chubb, she added, "What with him always popping off to London at the weekend, and his day off being different than mine, we hardly get a blinking chance to talk anymore, leave alone do anything else."

Mrs. Chubb clicked her tongue against the roof of her mouth. "I think that's just as well, my girl. Keep you both out of trouble."

"Yeah," Gertie muttered, lugging the tray over to the door. "Bleeding boring, that's what."

Before Mrs. Chubb could answer, the door flew open, and Ian stuck his head around the edge of it.

A bony-faced man in his late twenties, in Mrs. Chubb's opinion he was much too old and much too saucy to be paying attention to Gertie. But what the housemaid did in her spare time was her own business, as long as it didn't interfere with her work. Much to Mrs. Chubb's vexation.

"Hallo, love," Ian greeted Gertie with a cheeky grin.

Gertie dropped the tray on the edge of the huge scrubbed-oak table and answered with a squeal of dismay. "Ian! What'd you do to your face?"

Ian glanced at Mrs. Chubb and winked one eye. The other was already shut, swollen and turning an interesting shade of black. "Got into a bundle down at the George, didn't I? Full of them bloody workmen it was last night, all kicking and shoving—think they own the bloody place."

"Well, you're one of them," Gertie reminded him, screwing up her face in disgust. "Blimey, Ian, that ain't half a shiner."

"Yeah, but I live here, they don't. Always trying to pick on the locals, they are. Always looking for a scrap."

"Looks like you were more than willing to oblige," Mrs. Chubb remarked. "Let me see if Michel had any of that beef left over. Bit of raw meat on it will take it down."

She bustled out to the larder, tactfully leaving the two young people alone for a minute or two. Coming back with a slab of meat in her hand, she cleared her throat loudly before pushing open the kitchen door. Even so, Ian sprang smartly away from a blushing Gertie and gave the housekeeper another of his wide grins.

"Now, then," Mrs. Chubb said, slapping the piece of red meat on his eye, "tell me what happened."

Ian winced and pinned the beef to his face with his fingers. "I was practicing for the darts match with Dick Scroggins and the rest of the team, minding me own business, when they starts in on us. Well, Dick, being the owner like, was trying to keep it all down, but after a while he loses his temper and lets fly at one of them. Threatened to chuck the lot of them out, he did. Said he was sick of them causing trouble in his pub, and he was going to organize a protest march against the lighthouse project."

"Oo, blimey, I bet that did it," Gertie said, her eyes wide.

Ian nodded. "Right. Everyone knows how Dick feels about the new lighthouse, and the men working on it. Them Londoners are all the same, nothing but troublemakers."

Gertie snorted. "You was a Londoner a year ago, Ian Rossiter."

Ian reached out a hand and pinched Gertie's plump behind. "Not anymore, me darling. I'm a country yokel now, just like you."

Mrs. Chubb sniffed. "Well, all I can say is that you'd better watch your step, young man. You'll be losing your job if you're not careful."

Ian shrugged. "It's only for a few weeks anyway, then it'll be finished." He moved over to the housekeeper and put an arm around her pudgy shoulders. "Then, me old love, I'll be back at the Pennyfoot, brightening your days just like I used to."

"Here, not so much of the old," the housekeeper protested, but in spite of herself she felt her cheeks growing warm. No wonder he could turn Gertie's head. With those dark good looks Ian Rossiter could be quite a charmer.

"Well, I've got to get on," she murmured in an effort to hide her disquiet. She frowned at Gertie. "You've got half an hour to lay those tables, my girl, or you're going to be in hot water."

The housemaid answered with a resigned "Yes, Mrs. Chubb." She picked up the tray and looked at Ian.

"I got to go, too, love." He kissed his fingers and touched Gertie's cheek. "See you tonight."

Gertie merely nodded, and again Mrs. Chubb felt a twinge of anxiety. Usually the girl was ecstatic at the thought of being with her beau.

She waited until the door had swung to behind Ian's retreating figure, then took the tray from Gertie's hands. "Sit down," she ordered, ignoring the baffled look on the housemaid's face. "Something is wrong with you, and I want to know what it is."

To her dismay, Gertie's face crumpled like a failed soufflé. She sank onto the chair and crossed her arms over her stomach. "I'm bleeding late, ain't I," she muttered.

Mrs. Chubb blinked. "Late? For what?"

Gertie lifted her face, her cheeks looking hollow in her despair. "I ain't come on," she said, beginning to rock back and forth. "I think I'm bloody pregnant."

Mrs. Chubb's jaw dropped. "Good gracious, Gertie, you haven't . . . you didn't . . . when? No, don't tell me. Oh, luvaduck, you've gone and done it now, haven't you?"

Gertie promptly burst into noisy tears.

"Now, now," Mrs. Chubb murmured, pulling herself together. "That won't do. We need to put our thinking caps on here." She patted Gertie's heaving shoulder absently, her mind working on the problem. "Have you told Ian?"

Gertie violently shook her head. "Nah, he'd have a pink fit. I can't tell him."

"You didn't do this all by yourself, my girl. I think you should tell him."

Gertie screwed up her face again as fresh tears spurted from her eyes. "I can't, Mrs. Chubb. Not until I'm sure, anyway."

"There, there, now. Let me think." Mrs. Chubb gave the problem some more consideration. "How late are you?" she asked at last.

Gertie sniffed and wiped her nose on her sleeve. "Almost a fortnight. I think."

"You think?"

Fresh tears spurted from Gertie's eyes. "I . . . I don't . . . know. I can't remember."

"All right, all right. Could be you just missed one, that's all. We have to find out." Mrs. Chubb racked her brains, trying to remember remedies she hadn't used in donkey's years. "Gin!" she said suddenly.

Gertie heaved a shuddering dry sob, but at least she'd stopped that dreadful caterwauling. "What?"

"Gin." Mrs. Chubb hurried over to a corner cupboard and dragged it open. "I know Michel keeps a bottle in here somewhere." She pulled out a bottle of brandy and one of fine Scotch, then reached into the back of the cupboard. "Aha! I knew he'd got one hidden in here."

She turned, brandishing the bottle of colorless liquid, and found Gertie watching her with great interest. "We'll do it tonight. A hot bath and gin mixed with ginger. That'll do it."

"I've got to have a bath in gin?" Gertie looked at the housekeeper, doubt written all over her face. "What good will that do?"

"You sit in the hot water and drink the gin and ginger," Mrs. Chubb explained.

Gertie looked worried. "Strewth. I'll get sloshed."

"Maybe. But if it works, it will be worth it, won't it? It will stop you worrying yourself silly, that's for sure."

"What if it doesn't?"

The housekeeper sighed. "If it doesn't, we'll ask Madeline for one of her potions."

"'Ere, I don't want every Tom, Dick, and Harry to know I might have a bun in the oven."

Mrs. Chubb lifted a finger and wagged it slowly in Gertie's face. "If you have, then sooner or later everyone in the world is going to know."

Gertie slumped in her chair. "Bloody hell."

Mrs. Chubb replaced the bottle in the cupboard, then faced Gertie, her fists pressed into her broad hips. "All right, young lady, you can't sit there moping all day. Get on with them tables now. The more exercise you get, the better."

Gertie got up and picked up the tray. "Next time I come back," she muttered, "I'm coming as a bleeding man."

"Aren't we all," murmured Mrs. Chubb.

CHAPTER

3

Cecily found the trap ready and waiting for her when she stepped outside the hotel later that day. Dressed in a soft blue afternoon frock edged with white lace, she'd pinned a modest-sized hat on her head, trimmed with a single blue ostrich feather. Although no longer in full mourning, she wore a wide black band above her left elbow.

Since the sun shone in a clear blue sky, she took along her parasol and the six-buttoned kid gloves James had bought her last Christmas. She felt a quiver of pain whenever she wore the gloves. She couldn't forget Madeline's comment when she'd shown her friend the gift.

"Gloves are an unlucky present," Madeline had told her that cold, wet Boxing Day. "To receive them forewarns of a parting."

Cecily had paid no attention until a week later when James had taken to his bed with yet another bout of the

21

dreaded malaria that would not leave him alone. By the end of that month James was dead, buried in the churchyard of St. Bartholomew's just a few yards from where they'd been married twenty-five years earlier.

Shaking off the depressing memories, Cecily settled back in the trap to enjoy the view. Samuel, the new footman who had replaced Ian, sat stiff-backed in front of her as the horse's hooves clip-clopped along the Esplanade.

During the height of the Season, people filled the tiny street, gazing into the leaded bay windows of the shops or strolling along the ornate cast-iron railings that separated them from the smooth golden sands.

Now that the summer had faded, only one or two visitors hovered at the edge of the lapping waves, and a half-dozen more ventured along the row of shops.

The trap jogged the length of the Esplanade, then took the slope up to the High Street, where the villagers did their shopping. Here there were more signs of life, as the wives of the farm workers, tradesmen, fishermen, and businessmen bustled in and out of the shops.

Samuel tugged the horse to a stop in front of Dolly's Tea Shop and jumped down to assist Cecily from the trap.

Smiling, she thanked him, and added, "Please return for me in an hour, Samuel. I should be ready by then."

The young man touched his cap. "Yes, ma'am. I'll be here at four o'clock sharp." He climbed back up and with a flick of the reins nudged the chestnut into motion.

Lifting the skirt of her frock with one hand, Cecily stepped across the pavement to the door of the tea shop. A loud bang startled her, and she turned her head. Farther down the street, a bright yellow motor car chugged along, leaving a white cloud of smoke drifting around the red pillar-box on the corner. The driver and his passenger seemed oblivious to the noise as yet another loud bang exploded from the rear of the car.

Cecily looked at the woman seated next to the driver. She had a scarf tied around her hat to keep it on, as the draft in the open-top vehicle had to be horrendous.

Even so, Cecily thought, she envied her. It must be fun to drive at twelve miles an hour down the country lanes. She wondered what it would be like to go twelve miles an hour on a bicycle. Rather hair-raising, no doubt.

Turning back to the tea shop, she ducked her head to avoid the striped awning and pushed open the door.

A bell jingled loudly above the chatter inside, then jingled again as Cecily closed the door behind her. The room smelled of freshly baked bread, which increased her appetite.

A sturdy gray-haired woman she had never seen before stood smiling at her. "Can I seat you, madam?" the woman asked with a little bob of her head.

At that moment Cecily caught sight of an enormous hat the size of a tea tray, adorned with stuffed birds and surrounded by peacock feathers and pink tulle. The owner of the hat looked at her across the crowded room, lifted a gloved hand, and discreetly beckoned.

"I'm joining the lady in the corner," Cecily murmured, and the woman nodded.

"Yes, madam. If you'd care to follow me?"

Seated at the table, Cecily greeted Phoebe with a smile. "Have you been waiting long?"

"No, I arrived just a few moments ago. I've ordered tea for us both."

Before Cecily could answer, a buxom woman paused at the table. Her laughing brown eyes were almost hidden by the rolls of fat in her face, and her double chins waggled as she spoke.

Dolly Matthews had owned the tea shop for as long as Cecily could remember. The woman had seemed old when Cecily had been taken there with her brothers as a small child. It didn't seem possible she was still bustling around the crowded tables.

Dolly greeted Cecily warmly and introduced her to her new assistant. "Louise Atkins, she's replacing Maggie," Dolly explained, referring to her last waitress who had left to live in Scotland with her new husband.

This woman was much older than Maggie, but looked strong and healthy, Cecily observed.

Louise, it seemed, had come down from London in order to preserve her health. "All that smoke and dirt," she told Cecily, "it's no wonder people are dying of consumption every day."

When Phoebe asked the assistant where she was staying, Louise replied, "At the George and Dragon. Not nearly as elegant as the Pennyfoot, I'm sure, but it's the best I can afford at the moment, until I can find something more permanent."

"One of the Hawthorne Cottages has become vacant," Cecily said, tucking her parasol under the table.

"Oh, my, yes," Dolly said, her hand capturing her double chins. "Why didn't I think of that? Now that poor Mr. Bickley's a goner, the cottage will be empty again."

"It's in Hawthorne Lane, the road that winds up from the cove to Putney Downs," Cecily explained. "The cottages sit in a row overlooking the cove. A very pleasant view. I think you'll like it."

"Why, thank you, Mrs. Sinclair," Louise said, giving Cecily a charming smile. "I'll certainly look into it." She sent Dolly a quick glance. "If you'll excuse me now, I'll fetch your teas."

She hurried off, and Dolly watched her go, a slight frown on her face.

"She seems very capable," Phoebe said, her gaze following the assistant as she disappeared through the kitchen door.

"I hope so," Dolly murmured. "Good workers are so hard to find in these parts." She rubbed her hands together as if they were cold. "What do you think of that poor Mr. Bickley, then?"

"I didn't know the man," Cecily said, "but I imagine his sudden death must have been a shock to everyone who did."

"Used to come in here, regular as clockwork," Dolly said. She lowered her voice, which made it difficult to hear above the laughter and babble of voices. "Lying outside on the path, he was. Enough to give his neighbors a heart attack when they saw him, I reckon. Been there all night, they say. No one can understand why he was outdoors at that time of night without his coat."

"Perhaps he felt the heart attack coming on and attempted to seek help from the neighbors," Cecily suggested.

"I certainly hope it wasn't those little hooligans playing Knock Down Ginger who brought on the attack," Phoebe said. "Algie kept telling me they would get into real trouble if they weren't careful."

"Well," Dolly said, leaning her drooping breasts over the table, "he must have been frozen out there in his shirtsleeves, that's all I can say."

The woman seemed to have an inordinate interest in the man's lack of clothes, Cecily thought with amusement.

Her humor soon faded, though, when Dolly dropped her voice to a mysterious whisper. "They say the poor man was blue."

"Blue?" Phoebe repeated, sounding puzzled.

"Yes." Dolly shuddered. "Never seen anything like it, they said. His whole body, from head to foot, was bright blue."

"Oh, my." Phoebe clutched her throat. "I hope no one tells Algie that. He'll have nightmares for weeks."

At that moment Louise reappeared bearing a huge tray laden with wedge-shaped crustless sandwiches, scones, cakes, and a huge silver pot of tea.

"Well, I've got to get on," Dolly said, straightening as best she could. "Enjoy your teas, ladies, and have a pleasant afternoon."

Phoebe watched the rotund figure squeeze her way past the tables to the kitchen. "I don't know how pleasant an afternoon it can be after that piece of news," she murmured, one hand still clasping her throat.

Cecily smiled as Louise began unloading the plates from her tray. "Come now, Phoebe, don't dwell on it. Just look at these delicious little Viennese tarts, and that Swiss roll looks wonderful."

"I hope we have egg and cress today." Looking more cheerful, Phoebe plucked a sandwich from the plate and examined it. "They were all gone the last time I was here."

"These are egg and cress, and those are salmon and cucumber," Louise said, picking up the empty tray. "I'll return in a short moment with your hot water. I'm afraid I forgot to put it on the tray."

She hurried off, and Phoebe looked after her in surprise. "Her manner is a little strange, don't you think?" she murmured.

Cecily had entertained the same thought, but she said mildly, "It's most likely nerves. After all, everything here is strange to her."

"Well, it is most apparent that the woman is not accustomed to this kind of work. Not only did she forget the hot water, depriving us of our second cup of tea, but she also neglected to give us serviettes."

"I'm sure she will soon settle down. Now, while we're waiting, why don't we discuss the plans for the bazaar?"

Phoebe launched into a rapid account of the latest details, rummaging in her large handbag until she found the list of duties to be performed.

Cecily was examining the list when Phoebe muttered, "Well, it's about time. Wherever has that woman been?"

Feeling sorry for Louise, Cecily gave her a smile as she set the hot water down on the table. "I wonder if you'd mind fetching us both a serviette?" she said quietly.

Louise looked flustered. "Oh, I'm so sorry, Mrs. Sinclair. Do please forgive me. I can't imagine what I was thinking of." She rushed off again, missing Phoebe's raised eyebrows.

"Well, really," Phoebe murmured. "She is remarkably absentminded, though I can understand why Dolly hired her. The woman speaks very well indeed, and obviously she comes from a good family. Quite a treat to be waited on by someone well bred. There are so few places in Badgers End where one can be treated with the courtesy and respect due to upper-class patrons."

Cecily said nothing as Louise returned to the table once more and placed a folded serviette in front of each of them, then rushed off again.

Phoebe tutted, and shook out the large square of white linen. Placing it on her lap, she reached for her sandwich. "I suppose one should feel sorry for the woman. If one is to be widowed, the best one can hope for is to be left with the means of support. Thank heavens I do not have to work for a living. Dear Sedgely would never rest easy in his grave."

Cecily refrained from pointing out that "dear Sedgely" deserved a restless eternity, having failed to leave a will when he'd died from a fall while hunting. The Carter-Holmes family, having long deemed Phoebe beneath their station, had promptly disowned her and her son. It was Algie's meager salary as a vicar that kept their heads above water. Phoebe had seen not a penny from Sedgely's estate.

"Louise is a widow?" Cecily picked up a slice of Battenburg cake with the tongs and transferred it to her plate. She regretted the question immediately.

Phoebe leaned forward, her pale blue eyes glistening with the triumph of sharing a piece of gossip. "Her husband was a scientist. Traveled all over the world, so I'm told. There's something very mysterious about his death. He was in Central America, working on a science project, and was infected with this strange disease. No one seemed to know what it was. Can you imagine?"

Feeling uncomfortable, Cecily murmured, "Well, I'm quite sure there are many diseases in that part of the world that are strange to us. It could have been some form of malaria, such as that which caused James's death."

Phoebe looked abashed. "Oh, I do beg your pardon, Cecily. I think this might be painful for you. Shall I change the subject?"

Cecily had already decided to do just that. "I have something to tell you that should interest you. You have a secret admirer." She bit into the Battenburg, enjoying the almond flavor of the marzipan.

A look of astonishment blanketed Phoebe's face, and

color swept over her cheeks. "I do? And who might that be, pray? Not that dreadful Colonel Fortescue, I hope. The man is quite deranged, of course. I would suspect he could be dangerous if he weren't so completely ignorant. Then again, ignorance often can be just as dangerous as—"

"Phoebe," Cecily quietly interrupted, "it's not Colonel Fortescue."

Phoebe snatched up her serviette from her lap and dabbed at her lips, then began violently fanning her face. "Then . . . who?"

"Our new guest at the Pennyfoot. Sidney Rawlins."

Phoebe gave a small shriek, instantly muffled by her serviette. Her eyes looked wide and horrified above the white cloth, and the feathers on her huge hat trembled.

Cecily calmly went on eating her cake.

After a moment Phoebe lowered the cloth. "That man?" She'd uttered the word as if he were lowest of all animals.

Surprised, Cecily wiped her fingers on her serviette. "You know him?"

"Of course not. Nor do I wish to. I just happened to be in the lobby when he booked in. The man looks like a . . . a . . . Bohemian." There was no doubting the disgust in her voice.

Amused, Cecily nodded. "Yes, well, he is an artist."

"I knew it! With all that hair and those dreadful clothes . . ." Phoebe shook her head. "My dear, you really should be more careful who you allow on your premises. The man most likely never bathes. He must positively *reek*."

"Not that I've noticed." Cecily took a slice of chocolate roll, reminding herself to forgo dinner that evening. "Anyway, he requested that Baxter arrange an introduction to you."

Phoebe's expression of sheer horror was a delight to watch. "I presume that Mr. Baxter refused and put the man in his proper place?"

"Actually, Baxter said he'd oblige."

A strange gurgling sound came from Phoebe's throat.

"You know, of course, that heathen is merely after my money."

"You don't have any money."

Phoebe shot an alarmed glance around in case someone might have overheard. Leaning forward, she whispered fiercely, "He doesn't know that."

Leaning forward also, Cecily whispered, "Then tell him."

"I can't. I can't have people know that the Carter-Holmeses are not quite as wealthy as they appear to be. Such a disgrace. It would kill Algie."

Cecily didn't have the heart to tell Phoebe that her financial condition was common knowledge in the small village. Fortunately the villagers minded their own business and were much too concerned with their own lives to pay much heed to Phoebe's futile attempts at grandeur.

"Then tell Baxter you have no wish to be introduced," she said, still in a whisper.

"Why can't you tell him?"

Louise's face suddenly appeared between them, producing a startled yelp from Phoebe.

"Excuse me," Louise murmured. "I apologize for interrupting, but there's the little matter of the bill. Which one of you ladies will be taking care of it?"

Cecily reached for it. "Thank you, Louise. You can leave it with me." She could feel Phoebe's penetrating gaze from across the table. She hoped Louise hadn't noticed it. Phoebe's curiosity could be quite intimidating when one was on the receiving end of it.

She made a mental note to warn Baxter about Phoebe's reaction when she got back to the hotel. Perhaps it would be more prudent to discourage the artist from pursuing an introduction to her. Though secretly Cecily thought it could have been an interesting match.

Baxter had left on an errand when she got back to the Pennyfoot, and Cecily decided to go up to the roof garden to wait for him. She often went up there at sundown; it was her way of communicating with James.

The flat space between the sloping roofs provided a quiet

retreat and afforded a spectacular view of the Esplanade and cove. In the height of summer, the fragrance of roses, planted in gaily colored half barrels, filled the air. James had been responsible for turning the useless space into a small garden, to be enjoyed by everyone who stayed at the Pennyfoot.

But more often than not, he and Cecily had been alone during their brief quiet moments together, and she found the memory of him stronger here than anywhere else on the hotel grounds.

As she gazed out at the fishing boats anchored in the cove, she could almost hear his voice murmuring the sweet words that had kept their love so full of wonder and delight. Her thoughts of him no longer plagued her every minute of the day and night, but the ache of missing him remained as strong as ever.

The dismal cry of a sea gull echoed across the water, answered by another as it swooped low across the gentle waves. Already the night had darkened the horizon, erasing the line between sky and water.

The faint smell of seaweed drifted in on the cool evening breeze, and Cecily drew her shawl closer around her. In the early days after James's death, she had prayed for the memories to be erased from her mind. Now she found comfort in them. They were all she had left of a powerful love.

She watched the lights from the cottage windows flicker on, dotting the hillsides with cozy beacons of warmth. Soon the lonely night would be on her, reminding her of all she had lost.

Engrossed in her thoughts, she was startled when a soft voice spoke behind her. "Cecily? Can you spare me a moment?"

She turned, smiling when she saw the dark-haired woman who stood in the narrow doorway to the stairs. "Madeline. I didn't hear the door open. What brings you back tonight?"

Her smile vanished when she saw her friend's expression. Madeline's dark eyes were brimming with apprehension, and her face looked wan in the fading light. She came forward, her fingers plucking at the folds of her filmy skirts.

Her voice was little more than a whispering moan. "The spirits are against me, and that's for sure. I must have offended them, but I don't know why. Something dreadful has happened, and I don't know what to do."

Alarmed now, Cecily patted her friend's thin arm. "Tell me what's troubling you, Madeline. Perhaps I can help."

Madeline gave a trembling sigh. "I met Dr. McDuff in the High Street and inquired about Colin Bickley's death." She glanced over her shoulder to make sure they were alone. "He told me that Colin's death was not due to a heart attack, as he'd first thought."

"It wasn't?" Cecily felt a shiver of apprehension. She remembered Dolly's hushed tones as she described the color of the dead man's skin. At the time, Cecily had thought it was simply someone's exaggeration of a natural occurrence after death. But looking at Madeline's haunted expression, she felt a sharp uneasiness.

Lowering her voice, she asked quietly, "What exactly was the cause of death, then?"

Madeline gulped. "Dr. McDuff said he is sure that Colin Bickley died from some kind of poisoning."

"How dreadful. How the poor man must have suffered." Cecily still couldn't understand why Madeline should be so upset by the news—until she spoke again, and then it all became abundantly clear.

"Dr. McDuff said he thought the poison was cyanide at first, because Colin's skin had a blue tinge to it, which is a symptom of cyanide poisoning."

Madeline's hands twisted together like battling snakes. "But there was no smell of bitter almonds, which ruled it out. Upon further examination, Dr. McDuff decided some kind of poisonous plant killed Colin." She stopped wringing her hands and clasped Cecily's arm. Her fingers felt deathly cold.

"Cecily," Madeline said in a low, urgent voice, "Colin Bickley was at my house last night. I cooked him a meal, which he ate. A few hours later he was dead."

CHAPTER

4

Although Cecily had suspected as much, the words still shocked her. She grasped her friend's hands and held on tight. "Calm yourself, Madeline. There has to be some explanation for this."

"If there is, I would certainly like to know it. I swear to you, Cecily, I gave Colin nothing that I didn't also eat myself, and as you can see, I am perfectly well. But if he did die of poisoning, and Dr. McDuff seemed convinced of that, then I shall be blamed for it as sure as the moon shines above. Everyone knows I grow herbs and flowers for my potions."

Cecily gave the hands a little shake. "Come now, Madeline, let's not panic. What time did Mr. Bickley leave your house?"

Madeline seemed to have a little trouble concentrating.

She turned her head from side to side before answering. "It was a little before eight o'clock, I think."

"And he was wearing his coat, I presume?"

"He most certainly was," Madeline said, looking affronted at the question.

"Well, then, perhaps he visited somewhere else after leaving you. Since all the workers appear to congregate down at the George and Dragon every night, it's entirely possible that he joined them there before going home."

"He didn't say anything about going there." She pulled her hands free and raised them to her head. "Oh, great goblins, what am I going to do? How are the spirits going to protect me if they are angry with me? I knew when I heard that cuckoo that it was a bad omen. I should have paid heed."

"Madeline," Cecily said firmly, "I want you to go home now and try not to worry. I will make some inquiries and try to get to the bottom of this matter. Perhaps you can meet me in Dolly's Tea Shop tomorrow morning. I hope to have some news for you by then."

Madeline nodded, though her mind was obviously on something else. "I'll have to burn hemp and bindweed at midnight," she murmured. "Perhaps I should sprinkle a few horehound petals and redshank pollen for good measure."

"I think that's a good idea," Cecily agreed, hoping that the strange ritual would bring her friend some comfort. "Now I'll go down to the lobby with you. I have to find Baxter and send him on an errand."

Baxter was walking up the entrance steps as Cecily led Madeline through the doors and out into a brisk, salty sea breeze. She greeted him, then asked him to wait for her in the library. He bowed his head in acknowledgment, sent a curious glance toward Madeline, then disappeared into the lobby.

Cecily bade her friend good-bye with another word of comfort, and watched her until she had passed from view around the curve of the Esplanade.

She couldn't help worrying about her and with good

cause. Madeline had long been the brunt of superstitious tongues. This would not be the first time she had received blame for something that was not her fault. The death of a man was a serious matter, however, and as Cecily hurried down the hallway to the library, she prayed that she would be able to help her friend.

Baxter stood by the library windows when she entered, his back toward her. He appeared to be gazing out across the rose gardens, his hands clasped behind his back, rocking back and forth on his highly polished shoes.

When Cecily closed the door behind her, he turned, his face expressionless above his stiff white collar. He was an impressive figure in his black morning suit, and always held himself with an air of assurance that Cecily found most comforting. Particularly when she was disturbed about something.

"Sit down, Baxter," she murmured as she crossed the floor to the heavy table.

"Thank you, madam, but I prefer to stand."

It was the answer she'd expected. Ever since James had died, and she'd begun the habit of holding discussions with Baxter alone in the library, they had repeated that exchange. She invited him to sit down, he refused.

Baxter had never been able to hide his discomfort of being alone in the room with a woman, even if she was his employer. It simply wasn't proper, and no matter how hard Cecily argued that the world was changing and that certain proprieties could be eliminated, Baxter clung to the old traditions with the tenacity of a burr in a sheepdog's coat.

She dropped onto the chair with a small sigh. "I'm afraid that Madeline's indiscretions might have caught up with her." She pressed her fingers to her brow, willing away the headache that threatened.

Baxter waited, then when she didn't elaborate said quietly, "Madam?"

Cecily leaned back in the chair. "I don't know if you've learned of this yet, but apparently Colin Bickley's death was not due to a heart attack after all. Dr. McDuff believes he was poisoned."

Baxter raised his eyebrows. "Poisoned? By what cause?"

"That's just it. He's not sure. But he thinks it's some kind of plant."

A look of understanding crossed Baxter's face. "Aha. One of Madeline's potions?"

Cecily sat up straighter. "Oh, Lord, I hadn't thought of that. Madeline was concerned because she'd cooked the man a meal last night. Though she assured me he had eaten nothing that she hadn't eaten herself." She shook her head. "Surely she would have mentioned if she'd given him a potion."

"Not necessarily. It rather depends on the purpose for which the potion was to be used."

She looked up at him, but he'd centered his gaze above her head, as he always did when discussing a delicate matter. Cecily knew quite well what he meant. Madeline's business in potions did not consist entirely of medicinal cures.

Much of her transactions were for more personal purposes, such as the ability to attract the opposite sex and acquiring the necessary potency to follow through once one succeeded in the pursuit. Madeline guaranteed the success of her aphrodisiacs.

If she hadn't been so worried, Cecily would have smiled at Baxter's stony expression. "Well, we don't know that she sold him a potion. And there's always the chance that he called in at the George and Dragon on his way home, in which case it's possible he ingested the poison there."

Baxter cleared his throat. "It is possible, yes." But not very probable, his tone implied.

"We need to know if Mr. Bickley was there last night," Cecily prompted gently.

Baxter's light gray gaze rested briefly on her face. "You wish me to make inquiries, madam?"

"If you would, Baxter, please. Preferably as soon as possible."

He nodded briefly. "I'll leave at once."

"Have you had dinner, Baxter?"

"No, madam. I will take care of that at the George and Dragon."

"Ah, good idea." She waited until he was at the door, before saying, "Baxter?"

He paused for a moment, then turned to face her. She could see by his expression that he knew full well the request she was about to make. One of his eyebrows tilted slightly. "Madam?"

"I would very much like a cigar, if you would be so kind."

His eyes looked as if they could cut glass. "I do not think—"

"Baxter, if you would replenish my supply as I have asked, I wouldn't have to keep pestering you like this. Of course, I could purchase the things myself—"

"That won't be necessary, madam. I am quite happy to oblige now and again."

"Good. Then be so kind as to bring me some back tonight from the George and Dragon. I will see that you are reimbursed."

His voice sounded strangled when he answered. "Very well, madam."

"In the meantime, I would be most grateful if you would light one up for me now."

Cecily watched him go through the painfully slow process of extracting a cigar from the package and handing it to her, which was his way of establishing his extreme disapproval. All of which failed to faze her one tiny bit.

She leaned forward to accept the light from his match and allowed a puff of smoke to escape from her lips. "Thank you, Baxter."

"Yes, madam. I hope you suffer no ill health."

"Don't worry about my health," Cecily said, leaning back with a sigh of pleasure. "It's as robust as yours."

A faint tinge of pink colored his face as he turned away. "Do you wish me to report back tonight, or can it wait until the morning?"

"Tonight, if you are not too late. I shall worry until I know. If Mr. Bickley was there last night, it will certainly help to alleviate the suspicion on Madeline."

"One would most sincerely hope so." He paused in the doorway and looked back at her. "I shall not be late, madam."

"Thank you, Baxter. I'll wait up for you."

As he closed the door he gave her an odd look that stayed with her throughout the evening.

"Gawd Almighty," Gertie said, screwing up her face with disgust, "don't tell me anybody drinks this for bleeding pleasure."

Mrs. Chubb stood looking down at her, arms folded across her heavy bosom. "Drink it down, my girl. You've got a few more to go yet if you want it to do the trick."

Gertie sat in the steaming tin bath, her knees bent and sticking out of the water like pale twin hills. In her hand she held a tumbler full of gold-tinged liquid, the other gripped the edge of the bathtub in grim determination.

"If I knew I was going to go through all this, I would've told that Ian to keep his bloody hands off me," she said, scowling at the glass. "I'm going to be blinking sick, that's what."

"Nonsense. You haven't eaten anything today to bring up, so I don't know what you're worried about." That had been quite a battle, Mrs. Chubb thought, remembering the struggle she'd had to keep food out of Gertie's hands for the entire day.

"Yeah, and don't I know it. My stomach feels like a coal cellar. I hope I can eat when I've got this blinking lot down me." She took another sip of the mixture and shuddered. "No wonder they call it 'mother's ruin.'"

Mrs. Chubb edged around the tub and reached for the poker by the fireplace. She jabbed at the coals, encouraging the flames to dance higher. "You're not going to tell me that's the first time you've tasted gin," she said, opening the lid of the coal bin.

"Not with bleeding ginger in it, I haven't. Tastes like shit, it does."

"Gertie!" Mrs. Chubb straightened, a large lump of gleaming coal grasped in the tongs she held. "How many times do I have to tell you not to use that disgusting language? I've a good mind to wash your mouth out with soap."

"Probably taste better than this muck." Gertie took another sip. "Bloody 'orrible, it is."

"Well, you're not going to get it down you sipping at it like that. Take a good swallow. It will go down faster." Mrs. Chubb bent forward and dropped the coal onto the fire. She wasn't enjoying this any more than Gertie was.

Her tiny sitting room barely gave her space to move around as it was. With the bathtub in there she had nowhere to put her feet down. Even with her armchair shoved back against the wall, they could only just fit the tub in front of the fireplace.

Still, she could hardly let Gertie use one of the guest bathrooms, and the maids would be pounding on the door of the servants' one if Gertie was in there all night.

This had seemed like a good idea when she'd first formulated her plan, but now Mrs. Chubb wasn't so sure. She'd heard that the remedy had mixed results; maybe she should have asked Madeline for one of her potions instead.

But Gertie had been adamant about not telling anyone unless they were really forced into it. Mrs. Chubb watched as Gertie finished the mixture and loudly smacked her lips. "Does grow on you," the housemaid said, holding up the glass. "I think I can manage another one."

She actually managed three, by which time her cheeks were fiery red, her eyes were beginning to match her cheeks, and her speech had become thick and somewhat confused.

"Think I'll shleep here," she announced, waving the empty glass at Mrs. Chubb. "Can't feel me bloody legs, or me bot come to that. Pleash blow the fire out . . . no . . . need the bloody fire . . . water's cold." Her loud giggle ended in a hiccup. "Jush put the whole bloody thing on the fire . . . warm me up."

Mrs. Chubb viewed the housemaid's swaying naked body in alarm. Maybe she had overdone things. Gertie was built like a cart horse—it was going to be difficult to get her out of the tub.

She took the glass from Gertie's hand. "Come on now, my girl, you've had quite enough. If that doesn't do the trick, nothing will."

"I think jush one more," Gertie said, trying to hold her head up long enough to look at Mrs. Chubb.

"Not one more drop." The housekeeper grabbed the towel she had ready and held it up. "Can you stand by yourself?"

"Of coursh I can." Gertie struggled for a minute, but only managed to slide farther into the water. "Think I'll shleep here," she muttered, and closed her eyes.

"Oh, Lord Almighty." Mrs. Chubb dropped the towel and squeezed around the end of the tub. Grasping Gertie by the armpits, she heaved with all her might. The slippery wet body slid out of her hands, and Gertie shrieked with wild laughter.

"Oops-a-daisy, mind you don't bloody drown me, then." She hiccuped twice and closed her eyes again.

Mrs. Chubb tried in vain to awaken her, but no amount of shoving or slapping of wet skin seemed to have any effect. She couldn't just leave her there, the housekeeper thought worriedly. For one thing she'd catch her death of cold once the water cooled off. For another, it was entirely possible that she could slip under the water.

She wasted several more minutes trying to heave the limp body out of the tub, but Gertie's dead weight was too much for her. There was nothing for it, Mrs. Chubb decided. She'd have to get help. She would have to risk leaving Gertie alone and pray she didn't drown while she went and woke up Ethel.

With a last worried look at the now unconscious body in the bathtub, she rushed out into the hallway and down to the maid's quarters. Flinging open the door, she started to call out Ethel's name, then closed her mouth in despair when she saw the empty bed.

Who else could she trust? Gertie would be horrified if anyone found out about her predicament. Ethel was her close friend, but if anyone else on the Pennyfoot staff knew about this, the story would be all over the hotel by morning.

Dashing back to her sitting room, Mrs. Chubb assured herself that Gertie's head remained above water. If she didn't get her out of that water soon, she thought, the girl was going to catch her death of cold. She would have to ask for help from the one person who would not gossip. Madam.

On her way up the stairs to the lobby, Mrs. Chubb prayed she was doing the right thing. What if madam gave Gertie the sack over this? It would kill the girl to lose her job. Where would she go? What would she do?

Her face creased in worry, Mrs. Chubb rounded the top of the stairs. She now faced the main doors across the lobby, and as she paused for breath, they opened. A gust of wind swept across the carpeted floor as a tall, robust figure dressed in widow's weeds entered from the black night outside.

Mrs. Chubb believed in accepting a clear sign of Providence. Mrs. Parmentier had made it clear that she wished to be left alone. She had left instructions that she did not want her room cleaned, and when Gertie had taken up afternoon tea, the widow had taken the tray from her at the door, preventing her from entering the room.

She was obviously the type of person who kept herself to herself, and her nose out of other people's business. Perhaps she could trust her to be discreet, Mrs. Chubb thought hopefully. And since it was unlikely that Gertie would ever see the widow again after she left the hotel, the maid's embarrassment would be short-lived.

Mrs. Chubb started forward. She had no time to dither, since the widow was already striding across the lobby toward the stairs.

"Mrs. Parmentier?" Mrs. Chubb called out, grateful that the lobby was empty of guests.

The widow paused, hesitating for several seconds before turning slowly to face her.

Mrs. Chubb explained the situation rapidly before she could lose her nerve. She left out the reason for Gertie's dilemma, hoping that the widow wouldn't ask questions.

To her relief, the widow said nothing at all. Her face was hidden by the heavy veil, so Mrs. Chubb could only guess at her expression.

"We have to hurry, ma'am," she said urgently. "I left her unconscious in the tub and—"

Before she could finish the sentence, Mrs. Parmentier gave a sharp nod and swept toward the basement stairs. Sending up a small prayer of thanks, Mrs. Chubb hurried after her.

Gertie had slipped sideways, Mrs. Chubb noted when she opened the door of the sitting room. One arm hung outside the tub, the fingers lying in a damp patch on the rug. The housemaid's chin rested on her arm, and her loud snores filled the room.

Without a word, Mrs. Parmentier picked up the towel from the armchair, hooked it under Gertie's armpits, and bodily lifted the girl from the tub, wrapping the towel around her at the same time.

Gertie muttered an explicit oath of protest, then slumped against the widow's solid body.

"How did you do that?" Mrs. Chubb gasped, amazed at this display of remarkable strength and dexterity. Gertie was no lightweight, and unconscious she had to weigh a ton.

"I used to be in the medical profession," the widow said, her voice husky behind the veil. "Better get some clothes on her." Gently she lowered her burden into the armchair.

Gertie's head lolled to one side, but her eyes remained closed.

"I will, ma'am, and thank you so much," Mrs. Chubb said, hurrying to open the door. "I don't know what I would have done without you, for sure I don't."

"I'm happy I could be of assistance," Mrs. Parmentier

murmured. "I hope the young lady feels better in the morning."

Mrs. Chubb nodded, privately thinking that Gertie was likely to have a massive headache in the morning. "So do I, ma'am. And if I might ask, I know she would be grateful if you didn't speak of this to anyone. It would be most embarrassing for her."

"No one shall hear of it from me," the widow promised as she stepped into the hallway.

Mrs. Chubb watched her stalk quickly toward the stairs. Now that she really thought about it, Mrs. Parmentier did have unusually large feet. Rather odd woman, that.

Shrugging, she closed the door and surveyed the room. She had a huge mess to clean up before she could go to bed. As for Sleeping Beauty, once she got her dressed, Gertie would have to sleep in the chair. The housemaid would probably have a fit in the morning when she found out what had happened. How Mrs. Chubb hated dealing with bad-tempered staff.

Sighing, she fetched the large bucket and began bailing out the tub.

CHAPTER

❖ 5 ❖

When Baxter had still not returned from the George and Dragon by ten o'clock, Cecily decided to go down to the kitchen to make a nice pot of tea. She'd become bored sitting in the quiet living room of her suite, and was much too restless to read.

She had plenty of sewing to do—she was in the process of making new covers for the cushions on her chaise longue—but even that failed to relax her this evening. Her concern for Madeline had her nerves on edge, and the tea sounded like a good idea.

Perhaps Baxter would return in time to join her, she thought as she crossed the lobby. With any luck, he would have reassuring news for her.

She had just reached the head of the basement stairs when she heard her name called. Actually it was closer to a loud bellow. Reluctantly she turned to face the stout, ruddy-faced man charging unsteadily across the Axminster carpet toward her.

Colonel Fortescue was a frequent visitor to the Pennyfoot. He considered it his second home, which was nice for business but hard on Cecily's patience. The colonel had suffered trauma in the Boer War and had a habit of indulging in quite startling behavior when one least expected it.

Other times he appeared perfectly sound of mind, and as Cecily waited for him to reach her, she fervently hoped this was one of those times.

She could smell the gin on his breath as soon as he opened his mouth. "I say, old bean, bit of a filthy night out there, what?" His bloodshot eyes blinked rapidly at her, another affliction purportedly brought on by his narrow brush with death.

Cecily agreed, though the last she'd looked, the evening had seemed quite pleasant considering the time of year.

"Have to be careful of these dark nights, you know," the colonel muttered, glancing furtively over his shoulder. "Never know when the little beggars are going to creep up on you."

"Quite," Cecily said, not sure to what she was agreeing.

"It's Guy Fawkes, of course," Colonel Fortescue continued, his pure white mustache twitching like a squirrel's whiskers. "Puts the devil in them, by George. Never know where the damn ruffians are going to strike next. Dashed unnerving, I must say."

Cecily began to glimpse some sense behind the remarks. "Are you referring to the village boys, by any chance?" She wondered if the colonel had heard about Colin Bickley's unfortunate demise and had somehow connected the harmless games with the tragedy.

"What, what?" The colonel fished in the top pocket of his Norfolk jacket and pulled out a monocle.

Cecily watched in fascination as he fitted it into his right eye. It actually stopped the blinking on that side, though the left eyelid continued to flap up and down like an SOS signal light from a distressed ship.

Disconcerted by this odd one-eyed stare, she shifted her gaze to the grandfather clock in the corner of the lobby.

"Are you going to put on a show for Guy Fawkes?" the colonel demanded. "I remember last year well. Screaming fun. Could see the fireworks all the way across Putney Downs, so they say."

"I haven't given it much thought," Cecily admitted. "It's always seemed such a macabre celebration to me, burning an effigy of a poor, unfortunate man on a bonfire. Even if he did plan on blowing up the Houses of Parliament."

"Haven't thought about it? But it's the fifth of November next week. Can't ignore it, old girl. That would amount to sacrilege, by George." Colonel Fortescue was so dismayed his monocle popped out of his eye and fell to the floor. Muttering fiercely, he fell to his knees and began patting the carpet in front of him.

Cecily knelt down to help look for the small, round glass. The flickering gaslights cast shadows across the floor, making it difficult to see. "James always set up the fireworks display and set them off," she said as she stroked the surface of the carpet. "I don't think I could manage it on my own."

Her fingers closed over the narrow ribbon attached to the monocle. "Ah, here it is. Perhaps you should keep it attached to your pocket. Just in case you lose it again."

"Ah, yes, thank you, thank you. Pesky thing's a dashed nuisance. Can't see a thing with it stuck in the old peeper." He took the glass from her, then his expression changed as he directed his gaze to a spot behind Cecily's back.

"Ah . . . good evening there, madam! Awfully nice night out there, what?"

Cecily turned her head to see Mrs. Parmentier crossing to the stairs from the direction of the basement. The widow gave a brief nod in their direction, apparently unperturbed by the sight of the owner of the hotel on her knees with the colonel, who was grinning foolishly.

Wondering what the widow had been doing in the basement at that hour, Cecily scrambled to her feet and called out a hasty "Good night!"

Mrs. Parmentier lifted a hand in acknowledgment, then climbed the stairs at a fast clip.

"Fine figure of a woman, that," the colonel said, puffing as he regained his feet. "Too bad she's off her rocker."

Startled, Cecily looked at him. "I beg your pardon?"

"Oh, yes," the colonel assured her, his head nodding slowly up and down. "Quite doo lally, old bean. Tried talking to her. Would have none of it. Acted most strange. Most strange."

He shook his head sadly, his watery gaze on the widow as she turned the corner to the next flight. "Ghastly waste, that's what I say. Would have made some gentleman a spiffing wife. With those hips she could have turned out enough brood to fill a cricket team."

Cecily swallowed hard. She had to make allowances. And the colonel was a guest. She had to remember that. But at times it was extremely difficult to keep quiet. "Mrs. Parmentier is a bereaved widow. We have to respect her suffering."

"Oh, quite, quite. Didn't mean to be disrespectful, old girl. No, that would never do." Obviously flustered, the colonel dragged his pocket watch from his vest pocket. "Ah, I see it's time for a spot of cheer. Have to have the old nightcap, you know."

If he had much more, Cecily thought, someone would have to pour him into his bed. "I'll say good night, then," she said, starting to move off.

The colonel stopped her with a soft tap on the arm. Dropping his voice, he whispered, "Ahem . . . I don't suppose there's, ah, a card game going on belowstairs, by any chance?"

Knowing quite well that there were at least three card rooms occupied, Cecily looked him in the eye. "I'm afraid not. We don't get much call for that out of season."

He looked disappointed for a moment, then visibly

cheered up. "Ah, well, I'll toddle along to the drawing room, then. Might find someone to share a nightcap with me."

"I think that's an excellent idea. Good night, Colonel." Cecily smiled to herself as she went down the basement stairs. If he did but know it, she'd saved the colonel a considerable amount of money. He wouldn't have stood a chance against the kind of gamblers who enjoyed the amenities of the Pennyfoot Hotel.

She found the kitchen deserted, as was usual that time of night during the off-season. Filling the kettle, she reflected, as she always did, how much simpler it made things to have running water. When she was growing up, the water was drawn every day from the well, though she had no doubt it tasted better for not having been run through iron pipes.

She carried the kettle over to the stove and set it on top. The coals still glowed, and it took a matter of seconds to poke some life into them and then add a lump or two to bring up the heat. She had often thought how much more convenient it would be to have hot running water. But then, one couldn't have everything.

The kettle had just begun to sing when the kitchen door opened and Baxter poked his head around it. "Ah, there you are, madam," he said, coming into the room. "I thought you might be here."

"You are just in time," Cecily said, measuring tea into the large brown kitchen teapot. "Cup of tea?"

"That would be very nice. But please allow me to make it."

She sent him a reproving glance. "You know perfectly well that this is one chore I prefer to do myself."

He said nothing, standing by the door as if not certain what to do next.

"Baxter," Cecily said gently, "I do wish you would sit down. There is no one here to see, and I assure you it will not offend me in the least. On the contrary, it would be a good deal more relaxing for me."

"But not for me, madam."

She frowned at him, irritated by his stubbornness. "Very well, have it your way." She reached for the kettle and poured the boiling water on the leaves. "Would you care for a biscuit? I know Mrs. Chubb keeps some in that blue tin over there."

"Thank you, madam, but I ate a large Cornish pastie and two Scotch eggs. I think that is sufficient for one night."

"Yes, indeed." She crossed to the larder and found the jug of milk. Carrying it back to the table, she asked, "So tell me, what did you find out at the George? Had Colin Bickley visited there last night?"

"Yes, madam. According to Mr. Scroggins, the proprietor, Mr. Bickley arrived there shortly after eight o'clock and left there at half past ten."

"And did he have anything to eat there?"

"Mr. Scroggins didn't say. He was offended that I asked, and stated quite emphatically that many people had eaten at his establishment last night, and all were healthy today."

"That's as may be," Cecily said, pouring milk into two bone china cups, "but then the same can be said of Madeline's dinner, since she is also healthy."

She looked up when Baxter didn't answer, and found him watching her with an anxious expression on his face. "What is it?" she said sharply.

"Have you asked Miss Pengrath if she sold a potion to Mr. Bickley?"

Cecily thumped the jug on the table. "No, I haven't. But I'm seeing her in the morning and I'll ask her then. I must admit, the possibility of it worries me."

She lifted the lid from the sugar bowl and picked out two lumps with the silver tongs. Plopping them into the milk one at a time, she added, "There's something else, isn't there, Baxter?"

"Yes, madam."

"Perhaps you'd better tell me."

"I'm afraid there was some trouble at the George and Dragon last night."

Cecily filled the cups with tea, trying to ignore the

ominous fluttering in her stomach. She set the teapot down, then picked up the cup and saucer. "Trouble?"

"Yes, madam. There was a violent argument, which ended in a fight."

"Mr. Bickley?" She walked toward Baxter and handed him the tea.

"Yes, madam. According to Mr. Scroggins, shortly before he died, Mr. Bickley had been fighting with Ian Rossiter."

Cecily stared at him in consternation. "Ian? Surely not. Does anyone know why?"

"No one I talked to seemed to know." He took the cup and saucer from her. "Thank you, madam."

"It could have been something to do with Ian's job. But how foolish of him to fight with his boss. I thought he had more sense than that."

Cecily returned to the table and picked up her own tea. "I must say I am astonished to hear this news. I know Ian has a quick temper, but in all the time he has worked here at the hotel, I have never known him to engage in a common brawl. I wonder what came over him."

"Whatever the reason, it was considerably ill-timed, given what happened later."

"Yes, I see what you mean." Cecily sat down on a kitchen chair and sipped at her tea. "It's inconceivable to think that Ian would be capable of murder."

"He might not have intended it to be murder. He might have simply intended to make the man very uncomfortable."

"By deliberately poisoning him?" Cecily shuddered. "I find that impossible to believe."

Baxter stretched up his chin and ran a finger around his stiff collar. "I have to agree with you, madam, I cannot bring myself to believe that Ian is capable of such a dreadful deed. I am merely pointing out the suspicions that are bound to arise from the incident."

"Yes," Cecily said slowly. "It would appear that Madeline is not the only person to worry about." First thing tomorrow, she promised herself, she would ask Madeline about the potion.

The wind got up in the night, howling down the chimneys and rattling the windows in its fury. Cecily lay listening to the rain driving against the leaded windowpanes, and hoped that all the fishing boats had made it to safe harbor.

Two boats had been lost in winter storms early that year, and a freighter carrying goods from the West Indies had gone aground on the sandbank during the spring tides.

The lighthouse was sorely needed, especially in weather like this. Yet it seemed as if the project had brought trouble to the quiet little village of Badgers End.

Strangers had invaded the calm peace of the countryside, and it would be many weeks before the lighthouse was completed. Lying in the darkness while the storm raged outside, Cecily hoped with all her heart that neither Madeline nor Ian was involved in the death of Colin Bickley.

She hoped even more that there would be no more trouble at the George and Dragon. As Baxter had said so often, sometimes progress brings unwelcome changes. It would be a sad day indeed if the face of Badgers End, and inevitably the Pennyfoot Hotel itself, were to be lost in the never-ending quest for modernization.

Impatient with herself for her morbid thoughts, Cecily plumped up her feather pillow. The winds of change had been blowing ever since the death of Queen Victoria, and she welcomed them with open arms. Progress was good, for the people, for the country, for the world. She just hoped it wouldn't come too soon to Badgers End.

She left early for Dolly's Tea Shop the next morning. The wind had blown itself out during the night, leaving a carpet of dead leaves along the High Street and fluffy white clouds scudding across a pale blue sky.

The clean salty air carried a sharp chill to it, reminding Cecily that winter was just around the corner. As the trap bumped along the Esplanade, she could see the huge bonfire being built on the beach. On the night of November the fifth, the entire area would be lit up with the leaping flames, and the crackle and hiss of fireworks would fill the air.

The villagers would gather around the warmth of the fire and cook potatoes in the glowing embers, while waiting for the flames to consume the straw-filled effigy of Guy Fawkes.

A sudden stab of nostalgia caught her unawares, and she hastily turned her thoughts to a more pressing situation. The sudden and unexplained death of Colin Bickley. She could only hope that Madeline would be able to set her fears at rest.

She dismissed the trap with instructions for Samuel to pick her up in two hours. As she reached the door of the shop, two small boys confronted her. They held up grubby hands with a chorus of "Penny for the guy! Penny for the guy!"

Cecily dug into her handbag and found her coin purse. Taking out two large, shiny copper pennies, she pressed one into each small palm. "Don't spend it on sweets," she told them, smiling at their delighted faces.

Shouting their thanks, they sped off down the street in search of new prospects. Cecily watched them go, half amused at their excitement and half appalled at a custom that encouraged the children to beg for money.

A stirring of the cool breeze sent a shiver through her, and she pushed open the door of the tea shop to the welcome jangling of the bell and the fragrance of freshly baked bread.

She was enjoying her second cup of tea when Madeline arrived, breathless and apologetic, her cheeks flushed and eyes sparkling.

What an attractive woman she was, Cecily thought, watching the long, dark hair swing into place as Madeline sat down at the table. It was such a shame she couldn't find a man to love. Although she didn't know the full extent of Madeline's background, Cecily knew enough to understand why her friend had so much difficulty in forming a relationship.

Madeline had been fourteen, selling cut flowers on the

streets of London, when she'd been rescued from starvation by an elderly benefactor. The gentleman had taken the young girl into his home, and Cecily could only guess at what it had cost Madeline for her security.

Eventually, her "guardian" had died, leaving her penniless once more. Madeline had never married and had spoken only once of her past, and only to Cecily as far she knew. But Cecily knew her friend had never given up her yearning for true love, and probably never would.

Cecily waited while Madeline picked a tea cake to pieces before tackling the question she had to ask. Pouring another cup of tea from the silver teapot, she said casually, "Baxter went down to the George and Dragon last night."

Madeline paused in the act of wiping her fingers on her serviette. She didn't speak, but her eyes asked the question.

"Colin Bickley was there the night he died," Cecily said, replacing the teapot on the tray. "He was there from eight o'clock to half past ten."

Madeline dabbed at her mouth with the serviette. "Did he eat anything?"

"I don't know." Cecily folded her hands on the table. "I don't know that it matters. Anyone could have slipped something into his ale. It would have been simple enough to do without being detected."

Madeline's eyes grew large with horror. "Are you saying someone deliberately poisoned him?"

"We don't know. The point is that he was somewhere else, and could have been poisoned there, and that lifts the burden of guilt from you. Unless . . ." She watched Madeline's face while she paused.

"Unless what?"

"Unless," Cecily said reluctantly, "you sold him one of your potions."

CHAPTER
❁6❁

To Cecily's relief, Madeline's face registered surprise. "Of course I didn't. Why would he want a potion?"

"I'm sure he didn't. I just needed to know if you'd sold one to him."

Again Madeline's eyes widened. "You thought one of my potions had poisoned him?"

Cecily gave a decisive shake of her head. "No, of course not. But someone else might have thought so."

Now Madeline's face turned quite pale. "The police?"

"Well, let us hope it doesn't come to that. I'm sure once they discover what killed him, there will be a simple explanation for all this."

"And if there's not?"

Cecily helped herself to a tea cake. "I suggest we worry about that if the event occurs. In the meantime, tell me how the floral arrangements are coming along for the tea dance.

I'm not expecting too many people to attend, but I do want it to look nice."

Madeline launched into a somewhat distracted description of her ideas, and Cecily munched on her cake while she listened with half an ear. Her mind was still scuffling with the problem of Colin Bickley's mysterious death.

If Madeline was entirely innocent in this episode, could it be possible that Ian was involved? Surely not. Cecily had come to know the young man very well during his employment at the hotel. He had been most kind to her on more than one occasion during the first few dreadful weeks after James had died.

Although he had left the hotel to work on the lighthouse project, and she could hardly blame him for that since he was being paid far more than she could afford, she looked upon him as she looked upon every single member of her staff at the Pennyfoot—as if they were her own family.

With James gone, and her two boys in the tropics serving in the military, the Pennyfoot staff were all the family she had left. And, Cecily vowed silently, if Ian Rossiter was involved in this unfortunate and tragic situation, she would do her level best to help him.

"Cecily? Are you listening to me, or has a sprite whisked your mind away?"

Cecily started, sending a guilty smile across the table at her friend. "I'm sorry, Madeline, I'm afraid I wasn't paying attention. I was thinking about the preparations for Guy Fawkes and wondering if I should ask Baxter to put up a fireworks display."

Madeline clapped her hands in delight. "Oh, what fun. I'd love to help. That's if he'd allow it. Baxter can be so deplorably stuffy at times." She looked at Cecily with a mischievous grin. "Don't you ever get the urge to shock him a little now and then?"

"Frequently," Cecily answered dryly. She almost added that she very often did just that. But that was between her and Baxter, and it seemed disloyal to laugh about it behind his back.

Madeline's expression changed to curiosity. "Does he have a Christian name? All I've ever heard him called is Baxter. I assume that's his surname?"

Cecily nodded. "Yes, it is."

"Then what is his Christian name?"

Cecily felt uncomfortable. For some reason she felt reluctant to reveal that, though she had no idea why. To her relief, she was saved from answering by the sudden appearance of Louise, who had arrived at the table to clear away their plates.

"Thank you, Louise," Cecily said, smiling up at the dour-looking woman. "That was delicious as usual."

"Yes, ma'am." Louise stacked the plates and reached for the hot-water pot. "Will you be needing more hot water, ma'am?"

Cecily cocked an eyebrow at Madeline, who shook her head. "I don't think so, Louise, thank you. We would like the bill now, if you please."

"Yes, ma'am." Louise hurried away with the dishes, and Madeline leaned forward.

"She's not a very happy person, is she?" she whispered.

"She most likely doesn't have much to be happy about, since she has to work for a living."

"You and I work for a living, yet I would not say we were unhappy about it."

Cecily smiled. "I don't consider what I do in the Pennyfoot as work. It's more like taking care of a very large house. And Baxter takes care of the more troublesome duties."

"Speaking of whom—" Madeline said, then frowned as Louise returned with the bill.

"I wanted to thank you again, Mrs. Sinclair," Louise said, "for telling me about the cottage in Hawthorne Lane. I will be taking a look at it at the end of the week, on my day off."

Cecily graciously nodded. "I'm pleased to have been of help, Louise. I do hope you find the cottage satisfactory for your needs. It's a very pleasant lane and no more than a half-hour walk from here."

Louise managed a slight smile, then hurried off again.

"She's moving into Colin's cottage?" Madeline said, looking aghast. With her finger she sketched a cross in the air in front of her and mumbled something Cecily didn't catch.

"Is there a reason why she shouldn't?" Cecily asked, wondering if Madeline knew something she didn't.

"Well, of course there is." Madeline leaned forward again and hissed, "Spirits. Evil ones. They will be there for seven weeks after a death. Seven times seven nights. That woman is taking a severe risk if she moves in before they leave."

"Perhaps you can sell her something to ward them off," Cecily suggested, wondering why on earth she continued to humor Madeline's strange fantasies.

Madeline sat up with a look that said the thought hadn't occurred to her. "Well, I suppose I could." She gave Cecily a long look from beneath her lowered lashes. "That's if you are quite sure my remedy won't cause her more harm than good."

"Piffle!" Cecily picked up the bill with a flourish. "You know very well I never for one moment entertained the thought that you could have been responsible for that poor man's death. Now let's leave here before I give in to the temptation to take just one more tea cake."

She rose and led the way to the front of the shop, her mind already grappling with how best to help Ian if necessary.

"You don't look too well," Mrs. Chubb observed when Gertie staggered into the kitchen. "Perhaps I should give you one of my powders. Set you right on your feet, that will."

"Gawd Almighty, don't give me nothing else." Gertie uttered a loud moan and sank onto a kitchen chair. Her face was the color of sour milk, and she had black half-moons under her eyes.

"Well, you don't look well at all." Mrs. Chubb bustled over to have a closer look. She was feeling decidedly guilty for causing the poor child this much distress, particularly as it had failed to do the trick. Maybe Gertie was pregnant after all. Heaven help her.

"I know what I look like. I look like a blinking ghost, that's what. And if I bring up me guts one more time, that's exactly what I'm going to be. A blinking ghost."

"Now, now, the worst is over. You'll be feeling better in no time," Mrs. Chubb assured her, praying she was right. Gertie hadn't even begun her duties yet, and the morning was half over. Madam would be down wanting to know why the grates hadn't been cleaned and black-leaded.

"I ain't never going to feel right again," Gertie declared, crossing her arms across her stomach and rocking back and forth. "Blimey, Mrs. Chubb, you didn't half get me sozzled. And all for bleeding nothing."

"Well, we had to try, didn't we? Perhaps we should ask Madeline for a potion after all."

"I don't want no one else to know about this," Gertie said, lifting her head with difficulty. "You promised me."

Mrs. Chubb felt even more guilty. Deciding she had better say something, just in case Mrs. Parmentier happened to mention it, she said carefully, "I'm afraid someone else does know about it, dear. I didn't have much choice, you see. There you were, drowning in the bathtub, so to speak, and I couldn't haul you out on my own, so I had to get some help."

Gertie's expression changed to horror. "You didn't," she said hoarsely. "Did you tell Ethel? I'll have to nail her blinking lips shut if you did. You know what a tattletale she is."

"It wasn't Ethel," Mrs. Chubb admitted, feeling more awkward by the minute. "I did go down to her room, but she wasn't there."

"Thank Gawd for that." Gertie's relief was short-lived. "Wait a minute. Who was it, then? Not madam!" She said it as if Mrs. Chubb had told the King himself.

"No, no, of course I wouldn't tell madam." She didn't tell Gertie that she had been on her way up to do that very thing.

There was going to be enough pandemonium when she told Gertie the rest of it.

"So who, then? Come on, the suspense is bloody killing me."

Mrs. Chubb squared her solid shoulders. She was the boss here. She was responsible for the housekeeping staff, and as such she had done her duty as she saw fit. She had nothing to apologize for. Nothing at all. If anything, it was Gertie's fault for getting herself into this predicament in the first place.

Taking a deep breath, she said firmly, "Mrs. Parmentier."

Gertie's shriek almost split the housekeeper's ears. "What? Whatcha go and tell her for? Blimey, I don't believe it. I don't bloody believe it. Christ, the Black Widow herself."

At least the tirade had brought color back to the girl's cheeks, Mrs. Chubb observed with satisfaction. "Here, here," she said in an effort to reestablish her authority. "Don't you talk to me like that. I'll box your ears. You would have drowned, my girl, if Mrs. Parmentier hadn't dragged you out of the tub."

Gertie's jaw dropped open and the flush on her cheeks deepened. "She . . . what?"

Mrs. Chubb nodded with more enthusiasm than she was feeling. "Oh, yes, indeed. She was wonderful. Lifted you out bodily, with no effort at all. Just like that. Whoosh! And you were out." She demonstrated by lifting her palms straight up in the air.

"Good Gawd Almighty." Gertie sat up, her eyes growing huge in her flushed face. "Here, I wasn't naked, was I?"

"Starkers." Mrs. Chubb said unhappily. "What else could I do? I could hardly put your clothes on you while you were sopping wet and unconscious. You were slippery as an eel. I couldn't grab ahold of you."

Gertie slumped in her chair, her hands over her face, and moaned quietly. "I ain't never going to live this down. I'll be the laughingstock of the bloody village, that's what. What am I going to do? What the bleeding hell am I going to do? How am I going to show me face after this bloody lot?"

"Mrs. Parmentier would never breathe a word of this, I'm sure of it."

Gertie lowered her hands and gave Mrs. Chubb a look that indicated her disbelief in the widow's integrity on that point.

"Anyway," Mrs. Chubb went on, "it wasn't as bad as you think. She wrapped a towel around you as she dragged you out, though heaven knows how she managed to do that. She must be as strong as an ox, that woman."

Gertie groaned again. "Well, just don't ask me to take any more trays up to her. I'll never be able to look her in the face again."

"You can't see her face anyhow behind that veil," Mrs. Chubb pointed out, a fact that apparently failed to comfort Gertie.

"I think I'm going to be sick again," she said, and rushed to the sink where, much to Mrs. Chubb's dismay, she fulfilled her prophecy.

As soon as Cecily returned to the hotel, she sent word to Baxter's office that she wanted to see him in the library. He arrived shortly after, looking somewhat agitated.

She settled into her seat at the end of the table, and watched him pass the palm of his hand over his thick, dark hair. It was a habit she knew well. He always did that when he was disturbed about something.

His sideburns seemed to have turned gray overnight. She wondered when that had happened and why she hadn't noticed it before.

"I thought you'd like to know," she said, coming straight to the point, "Madeline did not sell a potion to Colin Bickley, and since he definitely consumed something after he left her cottage, even if it was only ale, I feel a little easier in my mind. Obviously he couldn't have been poisoned by the meal she served him, since she ate it herself."

"We have only her word for that." He stood just inside the door, as usual, looking as if he wanted to run out any second.

Cecily looked at him in surprise. "I hope you're not suggesting that Madeline lied to me."

"I'm not suggesting anything, madam." He shifted his gaze above her head. "I'm merely pointing out the questions the police will most likely raise."

Cecily felt a twinge of apprehension. "You believe they'll be brought in on this?"

"I think it's inevitable, given the circumstances."

She sighed heavily and gazed up at James's portrait. "What are we coming to, Baxter? First that terrible episode this summer with the deaths of two women right here in this hotel, and now this."

"The price of progress, madam. Even Badgers End can't stay excluded from the ways of the modern world forever, I'm sad to say."

Usually she would enter into a spirited argument with him on that subject, but her concern over this latest incident subdued her.

"I don't think you should worry too much, madam, until the results of the postmortem are known," Baxter added. "I understand Dr. McDuff is conducting the examination right now. No doubt he will ascertain the cause of the poisoning, which might very well clear Miss Pengrath of any suspicion."

Cecily nodded slowly. "I hope you're right, Baxter. I do hope you are right. But Madeline isn't my only cause of worry. This fight between Ian and Mr. Bickley could put Ian in a very uncomfortable position."

"True. But I still maintain that we must wait for the result of the postmortem before jumping to any conclusions."

She looked back at him and found him watching her. The concern on his face touched her, and she smiled. "You are right, of course, Baxter. I am most likely worrying about nothing."

When he failed to return her smile, she again felt a

moment's anxiety. "I see that the plumber has taken care of the problems in the bathrooms," she said in an effort to change the subject. "I'm sure our guests are delighted about that. Not to mention the maids. Emptying chamber pots is a task they've become unaccustomed to in this modern age."

She hadn't been able to resist the dig, but Baxter refused to rise to the bait. Worried now, she stared at him, and again he shifted his gaze to a point above her head.

"If that is all, madam, I have some duties I'd like to get back to."

"Of course." She hesitated, then, as he turned to leave, she added quietly, "Baxter, if there is something you're not telling me that I should know, I would be most annoyed if I discovered it later."

He paused, his back toward her, and she saw him stretch his neck. "I do not wish to worry you unduly, madam."

"You worry me far more, Baxter, by not telling me what is on your mind. You should know that by now."

She waited while he turned to face her, his expression unreadable. "There has been more news from the lighthouse project this morning," he said, rocking back and forth on his feet.

"More news?" She felt a flash of irritation with him. He had a very annoying habit of making her drag every piece of information from him piece by piece, as if by not volunteering it all he wouldn't have to tell her all of it.

"Yes, madam. Apparently there has been a spot of bother up there." Again he paused.

Cecily gritted her teeth. "What kind of bother? Not another fight, I hope?" A thought struck her, and she gasped. "Oh, Baxter, not Ian again, is it? Did he get into more trouble?"

"Not as far as I know."

"Then, what, Baxter? Would you please put me out of my misery and tell me what happened?"

"Yes, madam. Apparently someone has sabotaged the project. From what I understand, the work that had been done on the lighthouse itself has been destroyed. Most of the equipment has been either smashed to smithereens or has been pushed over the cliffs into the ocean."

Horrified, Cecily stared at him. "Oh, my God, Baxter, who would do such a thing? Why? What is the point?"

"I imagine the point was to delay the project for some reason. Apparently whoever was responsible achieved his goal. I understand it will be several days before they can replace the equipment, and weeks before they can repair the damage."

"I don't understand it," Cecily said, shaking her head. "The lighthouse is vital to the villagers. Most of them are either fishermen or make their living from working on the docks in Wellercombe. Who would want to destroy something that can only be a benefit to the village?"

"I have no answer to that, madam."

She narrowed her eyes as she stared at him. "Baxter, you don't think this has any connection with Colin Bickley's death, do you? After all, he was the foreman up there."

Baxter's intense gaze met hers. "I sincerely hope not, madam. If so, then it would raise a great many more questions."

"Yes," Cecily murmured, feeling a tremor of uneasiness. "It would certainly seem that the lighthouse project has brought bad luck to Badgers End. I wonder what Madeline has to say about that?"

CHAPTER

❖ 7 ❖

One of Phoebe's greatest pleasures was a brisk walk along the Esplanade, providing the weather wasn't too inclement, of course. It gave her the opportunity to dress up in the manner befitting her background, and as the mother of the vicar, she enjoyed a certain amount of deference from the local inhabitants of Badgers End.

This particular afternoon the climate was most pleasant, not too cold, yet cool enough to wear the mink-trimmed coat that had been the mainstay of her winter wardrobe during her marriage to dear Sedgely.

The light breeze was a blessing, since it meant she didn't have to worry about her hat. The extremely wide brim with its frothy cloud of yellow tulle and ribbon roses was inclined to slip loose from its moorings when buffeted by the wind.

Phoebe arrived at the entrance to the Pennyfoot Hotel in

fine spirits, and stepped daintily up the marble staircase to the huge double doors. She paused long enough to fold down her parasol, then pushed the doors open and swept into the lobby.

As she crossed the ornamental carpet to the huge, winding staircase, she thought about the many times she had visited the Pennyfoot when it had been the country home of the Earl of Saltchester.

Life had been very different then. So much had changed. Gambling debts had forced the earl to sell the mansion, and James Sinclair had renovated it, turning it into a very exclusive and elegant seaside hotel.

Phoebe hid a smile as she reached the foot of the stairs. Little did James imagine that his clientele would consist largely of bored aristocrats who were delighted to find a secluded hideaway not too far from the city, where they could engage in all manner of forbidden delights without fear of being discovered.

The Pennyfoot enjoyed a spotless reputation, thanks to the discreet staff bound by the policies set down by James Sinclair. Only the privileged few knew what went on belowstairs in the card rooms, or in the lavish boudoirs above them.

If Phoebe had not enjoyed a special friendship with Mrs. Chubb, she would never have dreamed that such goings-on happened in the Pennyfoot.

Not that she would breathe a word of it, of course. She was much too loyal to her dear friend Cecily.

Phoebe grasped the mahogany handrail and prepared to mount the stairs to the second floor, where Cecily occupied a suite. As she did so, she heard a discreet cough behind her. Turning her head, she saw Mr. Baxter standing there, looking most uncomfortable.

"I apologize for the intrusion, Mrs. Carter-Holmes," he said, "but I have received a request from a gentleman who is a guest here. He wishes to be introduced to you. He is waiting in the lounge, if you would care to accompany me there?"

Phoebe almost dropped her parasol. "I most certainly will not. I have no wish to make the gentleman's acquaintance, and I would be most gratified if you would convey that message to him immediately."

Mr. Baxter fixed her with a stare colder than a winter's sky. "Mr. Rawlins is a celebrated artist and a most honorable gentleman. I am quite sure you have nothing to fear from him."

Phoebe raised her chin. The hotel manager had a most intimidating effect on her, but she was determined not to let him know it. "Mr. Baxter, I have heard many stories concerning men who attempt to make their living by dabbling in the arts. I can assure you, none of them were considered honorable. Now, if you'll excuse me, I have pressing business with Mrs. Sinclair."

She turned her back on him and proceeded up the stairs as fast as her dignity would allow. As she reached the bend of the staircase, she looked down, and to her dismay saw the slender figure of the artist looking back up at her.

Her entire body became overheated, and she hastily averted her gaze. Her legs felt quite unstable as she climbed the second flight. The man was at least ten years her junior. She would feel flattered if it were not for the conviction that he was interested in her money. What else could he be interested in? And all that hair. Whatever would dear Sedgely say if he knew she was being pursued by a long-haired Bohemian with a paintbrush? Whatever next?

"I don't like to complain," she told Cecily a few minutes later, safely ensconced on a charming brocade Queen Anne chair, "but that artist person is really quite odd. It's enough to give me the vapors, the way he looks at me."

Cecily tried to hide her amusement. "I'm sure it's your imagination. He seems a very quiet, sincere man."

Phoebe tossed her head. "Really. Then pray tell me what he is doing pursuing a woman old enough to be his mother? He pestered Mr. Baxter to introduce us. Now, does that sound like logical behavior from a quiet, sincere man?"

"You are too hard on yourself, Phoebe. You are hardly old

enough to be his mother, and you are an attractive woman. It isn't all that surprising that a younger man would find you interesting."

Phoebe's flush indicated her pleasure in the compliment. "Thank you, Cecily, but I prefer the man in question would direct his interest toward someone more agreeable to his attentions."

She rested her parasol against the chair leg and took the cup and saucer Cecily handed her. "Thank you, my dear. A good strong cup of tea is exactly what I need. I really don't know what Badgers End is coming to. All these strange people about. It's the new lighthouse that is causing all this commotion in the village. I always said it was a mistake."

"Well, I'm afraid we'll have to put up with it even longer, now that someone saw fit to sabotage the project."

Phoebe nearly choked on her tea. "What is this? I haven't heard anything about it."

Cecily wasn't sure if Phoebe was more put out by the incident or by the fact she hadn't learned of it first. After relating what Baxter had told her, Cecily added, "At the moment no one seems to know who was responsible or why someone would wish to destroy something that is so badly needed. It seems so senseless."

Phoebe nodded slowly, sending the roses on her hat quivering. "Oh, I utterly agree. But at least one person I know of will be happy about the delay."

"Really?" Cecily murmured, her mind still dwelling on the possible motives for such destructive behavior.

"Yes, Dolly's new assistant. I overheard her talking to one of the workmen in the tea shop while I was picking up my cottage loaf and crumpets. Algie does love crumpets with his afternoon tea. Gets quite put out if I forget to buy them."

Her interest aroused, Cecily cut in before Phoebe could launch into one of her favorite anecdotes about the vicar. "You heard Louise talking to a workman about the lighthouse project?"

"Yes, I did." Phoebe sipped delicately at her tea before continuing. "She seemed most interested, wanting to know how long it would take, and asking if the men missed being in London. She said it would be very quiet in the village once the workmen left, and that village life was very dull compared to the city." She lifted her nose with a disdainful sniff. "I thought it disgraceful, a woman of her age."

Taken aback by this statement, Cecily put down her cup with a clatter. "Disgraceful? In what way?"

"My dear, that was a broad hint if I ever heard one. The woman was obviously angling for an invitation, and she didn't even know the man. I doubt if she was properly introduced."

"I'm sure she didn't see it that way," Cecily said mildly. "She was most likely simply making conversation. She's probably lonely, poor woman. She knows no one here, and I'm sure village life must be extremely difficult to get used to after living in London."

Phoebe replaced her cup in its saucer and dabbed at her lips with her serviette. "That's as may be, but I'm quite sure she could find someone more suitable to associate with than those rough laborers. For a woman of her obvious breeding, her behavior is quite extraordinary. I wouldn't have thought they were her class at all." She paused in the act of laying down her serviette. "You know, now that I think about it, she doesn't seem the kind of woman who would seek employment in a tea shop, no matter how refined it is."

"I don't suppose there is a vast choice of employment in a small community such as this," Cecily pointed out. She was becoming bored with the entire subject and decided to change it. "So how are arrangements for the bazaar proceeding? Have you got everyone organized yet?"

"Oh, that's the reason I am here," Phoebe said, reaching for her large handbag. "I have a list of things we desperately need, and I wondered if we could prevail upon you to loan us a few items."

"Of course, I'll do what I can. Let me see the list."

Phoebe withdrew a sheet of pink scented paper, crimped around the edges, and handed it to Cecily. "I do wonder, though," she said thoughtfully, "why someone like Louise Atkins would choose such an isolated little village like Badgers End to start a new life."

Cecily smiled. "If you were seeking peaceful solitude, where else would you look? Personally, I don't think she could have chosen a better place."

"Well, I hope she'll be happy here," Phoebe murmured. "It takes a long time to be accepted by the villagers. If it weren't for Algie being the vicar, I'm quite sure I would still be trying to establish my proper place in the community."

Cecily was much too diplomatic to pursue that topic. "Now," she said briskly, "about this list."

On her way down to the kitchen that evening, Cecily stopped by Baxter's office. She found him sitting at his desk, frowning over a large ledger. He stuck his pen back into the inkwell as she entered the room. Jumping to his feet, he reached for his jacket, which hung on the chair behind him.

He struggled into it and said a little testily, "I apologize, madam. I wasn't expecting a visit from you."

Cecily sighed. "Forgive me, Baxter. I should have sent you my visiting card."

A glint appeared in his eyes, but he chose to ignore her sarcasm and finished buttoning his jacket. "What can I do for you, madam?" he asked.

"I forgot to ask you last night. Did you by any chance purchase some cigars for me?"

He stared at her, defiance written all over his face. "Again, my apologies. I'm afraid I forgot your request in my concern to acquire the information you wanted."

"I see." Cecily pursed her lips. "In that case, I shall simply have to keep begging from you."

She almost smiled at the unhappy look on his face. "There was another matter I wished to mention. Phoebe tells me you attempted to arrange an introduction between her and Sidney Rawlins."

"I attempted to, yes. Mrs. Carter-Holmes made it clear she was not interested."

"So she tells me." Cecily hesitated, then decided to ask the question that had bothered her for most of the evening. "Tell me, Baxter, why do you think Mr. Rawlins is so anxious to meet her? Apart from the fact they appear to have nothing in common, Mr. Rawlins must be a good ten years younger than Phoebe."

Baxter's gaze shifted to above her head. "I fail to see the significance in that. I have never considered age to be a factor in a relationship."

"Really?" Cecily murmured, amused at this revelation. "Why, Baxter, you surprise me. I always considered you to be so conventional. I do believe you are a romantic at heart."

She watched a faint tinge of pink creep across his face and took pity on him. "Nevertheless, I would tend to agree with Phoebe that Mr. Rawlin's behavior is a little odd. He doesn't strike me as a Casanova."

Baxter cleared his throat loudly. "It makes little difference, if I may say so, since Mrs. Carter-Holmes has expressed her objections. There will be no introduction."

"That's a shame." Cecily turned to leave. "I really do dislike unanswered questions." She paused in the doorway. "Would you care to join me in the kitchen for a cup of tea?"

"Thank you, madam, but I have to finish these accounts tonight. I still have an hour's work ahead of me."

"Well, don't stay up too late." She left him alone to finish his task and headed for the basement stairs. As she reached them, she heard the main doors open behind her, and a draft of cold air cooled her ankles.

Turning, she saw Mrs. Parmentier appear in the doorway. The widow paused for a moment, framed by the blackness of the night behind her, then she pulled the doors closed with a loud thud.

Cecily was surprised that the widow had been out so late unaccompanied. In another ten minutes, the hotel doors would have been locked for the night, in which case Mrs. Parmentier would have had to summon someone with the night bell.

She wondered if she should warn the widow about that, but the stocky figure in black swept past her with the slightest of nods, unsettling Cecily to the point she felt reluctant to speak. It was difficult to communicate with a faceless person. She had never realized before how much one relied on other people's expressions.

She wasn't sure why, but she still felt a quiver of uneasiness, long after she'd finished her pot of tea and returned to her room.

Cecily found herself thinking about that feeling the next morning. She was in the kitchen, discussing with Mrs. Chubb the loan of six white tablecloths for Phoebe's church bazaar.

"Yes, mum," Mrs. Chubb said, "I'll get Gertie to fetch them for you just as soon as she gets back from the bedrooms."

Cecily was about to thank her when the kitchen door flew open and Ian bounced in. "Hallo, hallo, hallo," he sang out, then caught sight of Cecily and gave her a sheepish grin. "Morning, Mrs. Sinclair. Didn't see you standing there."

Mrs. Chubb sniffed loudly, as if warning him to watch his manners.

"Good morning, Ian." Cecily smiled back. "What brings you here? Aren't you supposed to be at work?"

Ian shrugged. "Project's on hold, ain't it? Someone did a right good job of busting everything up. Be some time before we're back in business. Matter of fact, Mrs. Sinclair, I was wondering if you've got a job for me around here for the next couple of weeks. Just till they get started up again, like?"

Mrs. Chubb, apparently outraged by this effrontery, exploded. "Of all the nerve. What do you think this is, young man, a charity house? You can't just drop in and out whenever the fancy takes you."

She sent a quick glance at Cecily. "Sorry, mum, but I had to have my say. Never heard of such gall."

Somewhat surprised by this outburst, Cecily wondered if Ian had upset the housekeeper in some way. She held up her hand. "It's all right, Mrs. Chubb. As a matter of fact, I need someone to do some painting around the windows facing the sea. They always bear the brunt of the weather from the Channel."

Ian shoved his hands into the pockets of his trousers and looked at Mrs. Chubb with a pained expression on his thin face. "Just for that, I shan't tell you the latest bit of news from the project."

Mrs. Chubb tossed her head in a gesture that said she couldn't care less, but his words caught Cecily's interest at once.

"Something else has happened?"

"Yeah, something horrible." For a moment his normally cheerful face wore a sober expression. "Somebody else dropped dead, that's what. Another one of the workers on the site, Billy Donaldson. Right outside the George and Dragon last night. The same as what killed Colin Bickley, they say. Dead as a doornail when they got to him."

Mrs. Chubb, her tiff with Ian apparently forgotten, clutched her chest and stared at him in horror. "No, never. Not another one?"

"Getting bloody frightening, it is," Ian said, edging toward the table where a large plate of sliced ham sat waiting to be taken to the larder. "Some of the chaps saw him die, and they said it was blinking horrible. Writhing all over the place he was, making terrible noises in his throat, like he was choking to death. He must have been in bloody agony, poor bugger. His skin was blue, too. Just like Bickley's. Makes you wonder who's going to be next, dunnit?"

He reached out a hand for a slice of ham, but Mrs. Chubb was too quick for him. She slapped his wrist away and glared at him.

"You work for your food here, young man. Don't you forget it."

Thoroughly disturbed by the news, Cecily wondered if Madeline had heard about it yet. She was bound to be distressed. "Did the two men work together?" she asked Ian. "Maybe there's something on the work site that's causing the problem."

"We all worked together, didn't we," Ian said, scowling at Mrs. Chubb. "There was Bickley, Donaldson, and four others as well as me on our crew. We had the hard part, clearing and leveling the land. Rock hard, it was. We had it looking right spiffy, but now all the brickwork is torn down and smashed to bits. It looks a right blooming mess again."

Mrs. Chubb clicked her tongue. "Well, if I was you, Ian, I'd watch what I was eating. Looks like something's getting into the food out there."

"Who supplies the food for the project?" Cecily asked, the same thought having occurred to her.

"All comes out of the George and Dragon, don't it," Ian said, giving the ham a look of intense longing. "Dick Scroggins gets the lunches packed up, and they bring them out to us on a hay cart. Then we all eat dinner there when we get back at night. 'Course, once in a while someone gets a sweet tooth and stops off at Dolly's for some currant buns." He sent a beseeching look at the housekeeper. "Come on, Mrs. Chubb, just one little slice? I am going to be working here for a while, ain't I?"

He looked at Cecily for confirmation, and she nodded. "Baxter will tell you what needs doing. Oh, and you might give John Thimble a hand in the gardens. He's busy getting everything cleaned up for the winter and could probably use the help."

Ian nodded cheerfully. "Thanks, Mrs. Sinclair. Now, about that ham?"

Cecily smiled at Mrs. Chubb. "I don't think a sandwich would hurt, Mrs. Chubb. At least we know our food is safe to eat."

"Yeah, well, we'll soon find out if it is something in the food from the George," Ian said as Mrs. Chubb reluctantly took a loaf of crusty bread out of the bin. "The bobbies are on the case now. They've called in Inspector Cranshaw from Wellercombe. I was told on the quiet like that they don't think it was an accident. Not to happen twice like that. They think it's murder."

He gave a satisfied grin at Mrs. Chubb's horrified gasp. "How about that, me old duck?" He gave a menacing, hollow laugh. "Maybe Jack the Ripper's hiding out in Badgers End."

CHAPTER

8

"I hardly think it's likely that Jack the Ripper is responsible for the poisonings," Cecily said firmly, taking a look at Mrs. Chubb's terrified expression. "For one thing, he killed with a knife, and for another, his victims were women, usually of ill repute. I doubt if a man like that would find much to interest him in Badgers End."

"Oh, my, I certainly would hope not," Mrs. Chubb said fearfully. "I'd never sleep easy in my bed again if I thought that horrible monster was anywhere near here."

Ian laughed. "Well, me old love, all I can say is, it's a good job our murderer doesn't take a fancy to widows. What with you and Mrs. Sinclair, and Mrs. Carter-Holmes, then there's that new waitress at Dolly's, and the one who's staying here who Gertie calls the Black Widow . . ." He chuckled again. "The bloke would have plenty to pick from, right enough."

"Ian Rossiter!" Mrs. Chubb lifted the bread knife and wagged it at him. "If you want this sandwich, you'll mind your manners this instant."

Apparently realizing he might have gone too far, Ian sent Cecily a sheepish look. "I didn't mean no disrespect, Mrs. Sinclair."

"That's all right, Ian." Cecily moved to the door. "Finish your sandwich, then you'll find Baxter in his office." She left the kitchen, leaving a disgruntled-looking housekeeper wielding the bread knife on a large, crusty loaf.

Cecily had known Dr. McDuff since the day she was born. The good doctor had not only brought her safely into the world, but every one of her five brothers as well. With her parents and two of her brothers dead, two brothers serving abroad in the military, and one raising sheep in New Zealand, Cecily was the only member of the family still living in Badgers End.

Dr. McDuff was long past the age of retirement, but swore that until he could no longer ride his bicycle, he would remain in practice.

There were times when Cecily saw him pedaling unsteadily up the hill to Putney Downs when she felt that moment was not far off. Yet here was another winter, and still the gruff doctor managed his rounds.

He greeted Cecily that afternoon with his usual boisterous laugh, his fierce, shaggy eyebrows as white as summer clouds above the faded blue eyes. "What brings you here, lassie, on such a fine day?" he demanded, his once-strong brogue diluted by years of living south of the border. "Are ye not well, then?"

"I'm feeling a little peaky," Cecily said, uncomfortable at using the subterfuge with such an old friend. But she knew full well that had he known the real reason for her visit, Gordon McDuff would have clamped his mouth shut, after telling her to mind her own business.

The doctor's fingers strayed to his short, clipped beard.

"Will ye be needing a tonic, then, is that it? Or is it something more serious?"

"I think a tonic will do the trick." Cecily smiled at him. "Probably just a case of winter depression."

"Aye, 'tis understandable. All the same, I'd like to take a wee look down your throat, just to be sure."

Cecily obediently opened her mouth and let the doctor shine a light down her throat. After listening to her say "Ah" a couple of times, he gently pulled down her lower eyelids, poked around in her ears, laid the back of his hand against her forehead, then diagnosed a mild case of tired blood.

"Take a tablespoon twice a day for a week," he said, scribbling on his prescription pad, "and you'll be as good as new."

"Thank you," Cecily said, taking the folded piece of paper. "I'll call in at the chemist's on the way home." She tucked the prescription into the pocket of her cape, then settled back in her chair.

"You have had a most unusual week," she said, "with two deaths in the space of two days."

Dr. McDuff looked at her suspiciously across his desk, which was strewn with various packages, bottles, and pieces of literature. A half-eaten apple rested on the cover of a heavy leather-bound tome, and a glass half-full of some pink-colored liquid sat next to it.

"This is police business now, ye know," he said, tapping his fingers on the edge of the glass. "So don't be asking me any questions I canna answer."

"I wouldn't dream of it." Cecily pulled a scented handkerchief from her pocket and dabbed at her nose. She had always hated the smell of the doctor's surgery. Growing up with five robust brothers, she had usually come off the worse for wear during their many escapades, and had spent many hours being patched up by the doctor.

His caustic comments while painting her cuts and bruises with iodine had done nothing to soothe her injured pride, and the smell of disinfectant reminded her of those painful times.

"I do understand, though," she added, "that both men died of poisoning. I believe that is common knowledge in the village."

"Aye, it is." The doctor's eyebrows joined together. "And that's all I have to say on the subject."

"Of course. Though I understand from Madeline that you believe the cause was a poisonous plant. Something that turns the skin blue?"

Dr. McDuff spread his hands in appeal. "I gave that information to Madeline before I knew it was police business. You know I canna talk about this now."

"Dr. McDuff," Cecily said earnestly, "Madeline is my friend. She is afraid that she might be considered a suspect in the poisoning. Now that the police are involved, I feel that her fears are well founded. I need to know all I can in order to help her. If there's anything you can tell me that will help me do that, I can promise you it won't go any further."

She waited anxiously as the doctor stared at her, his fingers tapping busily on the glass.

"I can tell you this," he said at last. "I have gone through my records thoroughly. There are two plants that cause similar symptoms to cyanide poisoning and leave the skin with a tinge of blue after death. The hydrangea and the larkspur. After studying the symptoms and the results from the postmortem examinations, I have ruled out the hydrangea."

Cecily caught her breath. The distinctive blue flowers of the larkspur grew in profusion in Madeline's garden. "Well," she said, looking the doctor straight in the eye, "I'm sure those plants grow in any number of gardens in the village. I really don't think Madeline can be considered a suspect on such feeble evidence."

"Not on its own, granted," Dr. McDuff said, his eyes full of concern. "But I'm sure you know she was very well acquainted with both men. In fact, so I believe, Mr. Bickley dined at her house the night he died."

The fact that Madeline had also known the second dead man came as a nasty surprise to Cecily. Nevertheless, she managed to appear unaffected by the news. "And both men died after leaving the George and Dragon. Anyone could have slipped the poison into their beer."

"That is feasible," the doctor agreed. "But unlikely. According to my research, the symptoms occur immediately after ingesting the poison. Both men died of the same poison. Billy Donaldson died immediately after leaving the pub. Yet Colin Bickley was seen returning to his cottage late that night by two of his neighbors, both of whom attested that he appeared perfectly normal, and that was after a good thirty-minute walk."

He dropped his gaze and fidgeted with the glass. "I have to ask, lassie, that if both men drank the same poison in their beer while at the pub, why did it take Bickley so long to die?"

Cecily was not about to give up. "If that's the case, then Mr. Bickley could not have been poisoned at Madeline's house, since he went to the pub after leaving her."

"Aye." Dr. McDuff turned his tired gaze on Cecily again. "But Madeline uses the flowers in her gardens for those useless remedies she peddles to the poor fools who believe in all that mumbo jumbo nonsense. If she sold the same potion to Donaldson and Bickley, and they took them at different times, that would explain the discrepancy in the time of death. Do ye not see that?"

Cecily saw that very well. Baxter had already mentioned the possibility. But Madeline had denied ever selling a potion to Colin Bickley. And Cecily believed her. She knew full well the futility of arguing the point with the doctor, however. As a man of science, naturally he viewed Madeline's "witchcraft" with the utmost contempt.

"All I hope is that the police do a thorough investigation before jumping to unfortunate conclusions." She stood, smoothing down the folds of her dark blue skirt.

"I know how you feel about Madeline," Dr. McDuff said, standing also. "But it is very dangerous to play around with flowers and such, especially when you start mixing them into stuff for people to drink. So many of them are deadly poison. It's a blessed miracle she hasn't killed someone before this."

"Dr. McDuff," Cecily said firmly, "as far as the law is concerned, Madeline is innocent until proven guilty. I hope you will remember that."

"I will, lassie, I will. But I have to report my findings to the police. Inspector Cranshaw is sending a trap for me this afternoon."

Cecily's spirits plummeted. That didn't give her much time. "Just tell me one more thing," she said as she reached the door. "Did the two men have anything in common, other than the fact they worked together?"

Dr. McDuff stroked his beard. "Now you come to mention it, they were about the same age and had similar coloring. From what I hear, they both enjoyed spending time with the ladies and had plenty of chances. They were both fine-looking men. What a terrible waste of young manhood."

"But that's all?" Cecily asked, not quite sure what she was hoping to hear.

"Well, they did have one more thing in common," the doctor said quietly. "They were both courting Madeline Pengrath."

That, Cecily thought as she left the surgery, was the most damning evidence of all.

"Now look sharp with this sandwich," Mrs. Chubb said, smearing a thick layer of hot mustard on the ham. "I want you out of here before Gertie gets back. I don't need you disrupting her from her work."

She shoved the plate at Ian and stomped over to the sink to wash her hands.

"Thanks, me old duck," he said behind her.

"Don't thank me, thank madam. She treats you better than you deserve, in my opinion."

She turned to face him, drying her hands on a tea towel, and found him gazing at her, a hurt expression on his face.

"Have I done something to upset you, love?"

Mrs. Chubb had to bite her tongue to keep from telling

him exactly what he had done. "You're holding up my work, that's what," she said, looking up at the big kitchen clock on the mantel. "Michel will be here any minute to start lunch, and you know how he hates anyone in his kitchen when he's working."

"All bloody chefs are alike," Ian mumbled, his mouth full of ham sandwich. "They all got a blooming high opinion of themselves."

"Who's got a blooming high opinion of theirselves?" Gertie said from the doorway.

Ian turned with a grin. "Hallo, me darling, you look as pretty as a picture, I do say."

Gertie pulled a face at him. "You'd say that even if I looked blinking horrible," she said, crossing the floor with an armload of bottles and rags.

Mrs. Chubb was inclined to agree with her. Gertie looked far from well, with a pasty complexion and those dark circles around her eyes. She was dying to say something, but it was none of her business, and far be it for Altheda Chubb to poke her nose in where it wasn't wanted.

"I'm off on my tour of inspection," she said, depositing the bread knife in the sink to be washed. "And by the way, Gertie, madam informed me that the chimney sweeps will be here on Thursday. So you and Ethel will have to get busy putting the covers out on the empty rooms."

"Yes, Mrs. Chubb," Gertie said far too complacently. She opened the cupboard under the sink and stowed away the cleaning supplies.

As she straightened up, Mrs. Chubb gave her a searching look. "Don't hang around talking too long, then, not unless you've got something important to say, that is."

The flash of warning from Gertie's dark eyes assured Mrs. Chubb she'd understood the subtle hint. Hoping the housemaid would take her advice and tell Ian about her problem, Mrs. Chubb left them alone.

The minute the door closed behind her, Ian grabbed Gertie about the waist and gave her a squeeze.

Deftly Gertie stepped away from him and put the table

between them. "I've got a lot on me plate today, Ian, so you'd best be off. Aren't you late for work, anyhow?"

With an expression of hurt surprise, Ian shook his head. "Nah, it's closed down, ain't it. Have I done something wrong? Mrs. Chubb's been acting strange, and now you're giving me the cold shoulder. What did I do?"

Gertie managed a smile. "Nothing. Honest. I just got a blinking lot of work to do, that's all. So what are you going to do, then, if you can't go to work?"

"I'm going to work here, ain't I. Mrs. Sinclair gave me a job till I can get back on the lighthouse project. She's a bit of all right, that lady."

He peered at Gertie's face. "You don't look too happy at the news. I thought you'd be pleased as punch to have me around a bit more. You made enough blooming fuss when I told you I was leaving."

Gertie shrugged. "'Course I'm happy. But all this upset about someone smashing up the lighthouse gives me the willies, it does."

"Yeah? Well I'll tell you something else that'll give you the willies." Ian edged around the corner of the table. "Someone else dropped dead outside the G and D last night."

"Go on! Who was it, then?"

"Billy Donaldson. Died of poison, the same way as Bickley. Turned blue, he did."

Gertie stared at him in horror. "Gawd Almighty. Billy? He was such a nice, friendly bloke. And no older than you. What's going on, then?"

"The police think it's murder," Ian said with a certain amount of relish.

Gertie felt sick. Actually she'd been feeling sick ever since she got up that morning, but this news made her feel a great deal worse. "Bloody hell. Is it the same person what did all that damage up at the lighthouse?"

"Don't know." Ian finished the last piece of his sandwich and licked his fingers. "If I tell you a secret, will you swear not to tell a living soul?"

There was nothing in the world Gertie liked more than being entrusted with a secret. She enjoyed the prestige it gave her when she knew something no one else was supposed to know. Especially when she told someone that.

"'Course I won't," she said, which in her eyes didn't exactly amount to a solemn promise not to tell.

"Well, I think I know who it was who did all that mess up at the project."

Gertie almost stopped breathing. This was better than she could have imagined. It almost made her forget her own nagging worry about being late with the curse. "Go on," she urged, moving closer to Ian so she wouldn't miss a word of what he said. "Tell me. Who was it, then?"

Ian cast a furtive glance at the closed kitchen door, then dropped his voice to a whisper. "I think it was Dick Scroggins."

Gertie was so surprised she forgot to whisper. "Dick Scroggins?"

Ian pressed a finger against her lips. "Shh. I told you it was a secret."

Gertie jerked her head back. In a fierce whisper she said, "You must be bleeding daft. Dick Scroggins owns the George. Why would he want to mess up something that's giving him all that business?"

"Because," Ian said quietly, "he's got a smuggling run from France, bringing in brandy for the pub. Once that light goes on in the lighthouse, them cliffs will be lit up like the seafront at Blackpool. He'll never get his boats in without being seen."

"How'd you know all this if it's such a bloody big secret?" Gertie demanded, unable to believe she'd been handed such a prize piece of confidential information.

Ian laid a finger along his nose. "Ah, well, that would be telling, wouldn't it?"

Gertie stared at him, a growing suspicion forming in her astonished mind. "Bleeding hell, Ian Rossiter. You was in it with him, wasn't you? You've been blinking smuggling, I know you have."

Ian sent a nervous glance at the door. "That's why you got to keep your mouth shut, Gertie. If word of this gets out, I'll be in dead trouble, I will. I'll go to the nick, then the only way you'll see me is through bars."

Gertie thought of the seed possibly growing inside her and reluctantly abandoned the pleasure of divulging the secret. If she was bloody pregnant, she told herself, she was going to make sure that Ian Rossiter did the right thing and stood by her.

He might not be exactly what she'd choose to marry, if she chose to marry at all, but sometimes you had to grab your chances where they lay, so to speak. And she was bloody sure she wasn't going to be left out on the streets with a bun in the oven.

"All right, I won't tell. But you better hope it ain't him. 'Cos if the police pick him up, they'll round up everyone who was in it with him." She frowned, the full impact of what she'd said finally penetrating. "Here, you don't think he did the poisoning, too, do you?"

Again Ian shrugged. "How the hell do I know? I tell you what, though. I sure as blazes ain't going to eat anything else what comes out of the G and D. Not if I was blooming starving, I wouldn't."

"Gawd," Gertie whispered, awed by the enormity of what she'd just heard. "Me neither."

CHAPTER 9

Colonel Fortescue greeted Cecily at the top of the steps when she returned to the hotel. "See the rain's keeping off, old bean," he said, looking up at the clouds buffeting each other overhead. "Hope it stays dry for Guy Fawkes. Dashed difficult to light wet firewood, you know. I remember once, when I was in India . . ."

He held the door open for Cecily, and she thanked him as she walked into the lobby. He followed her, still talking.

". . . couldn't get the blighter to catch. Wasted a whole box of matches on the pesky thing. Lots of chaps drinking at the time. Some dashed awful stuff they'd filched from the natives. Started chucking the glasses over their shoulders at the fireplace, shouting 'The Queen!' when the glasses smashed to smithereens."

Cecily nodded, only half listening. She was anxious to talk to Baxter about what she'd learned from Dr. McDuff.

Somehow she could think more clearly when she discussed her problems with him.

"Anyway," the colonel went on, "half the chaps were chucking the booze away with the glasses. Soaked the firewood, of course. Then someone got excited and fired a shot into the grate. Whole damn thing went up like Vesuvius. Never saw so many drunks move so fast in all my life—"

"Colonel," Cecily began, but he was off and running, and short of rudely walking away from him, she was trapped for the time being.

"Just came back from a game of bowls," the colonel boomed, twirling his mustache. "Played a spiffing game, if I say so myself."

"How very nice," Cecily murmured. "Now, if you'll excuse me—"

"I say, old bean. What's all this about two chappies being poisoned? Lots of talk about it on the bowling green. Turned blue, what? What?"

Cecily sighed. "So I hear. But I'm afraid I—"

"Reminds me of the time I saw a chap turn blue. Was out in the tropics at the time. Damn sticky wicket that was. Went down like a felled elephant. Died right where he stood, they said. One minute he was chipper, the next he was writhing on the ground. Excruciating agony, old bean. Never saw anything like it in my life—"

Across the lobby Cecily caught sight of Baxter, striding toward the basement steps. He glanced in her direction, and she wagged her eyebrows up and down at him in a frantic plea for help.

"Carried him off on a stretcher made of bamboo, poor blighter. Too short for him, it was. Always remember his head—"

"Oh, excuse me, madam," Baxter said loudly, striding across the carpet toward her. "I'm afraid there is some kind of emergency in the kitchen. It needs your immediate attention, so I believe."

"Of course, Baxter," Cecily said, giving him a relieved smile. "Do please forgive me, Colonel Fortescue?"

"Yes, yes, dear lady, of course. Hope it isn't anything too drastic, what? What?"

"I'm sure it's something I can handle." With a smiling nod at the colonel, she hurried across the lobby to follow Baxter down the steps.

He paused at the kitchen door and looked back at her. "I trust I did the right thing, madam?"

"You most certainly did," Cecily assured him, breathing a little hard from her hurried descent. "I swear, one of these fine days I am going to tell the colonel exactly what an old bore he is."

Baxter pursed his lips. "I doubt that, madam."

She grinned at him. "You know me well. Are you in a rush, Baxter? I have something I would like to discuss with you. In the library, if you have time?"

"I will be there shortly, madam."

"Fine, I'll wait for you." She turned to go, then looked back at him. "Oh, and, Baxter, do bring your cigars, will you, please?" She didn't wait to see his look of reproof.

The library offered a few minutes' respite from her churning thoughts. Standing in front of James's portrait, she looked at the image of her handsome husband and felt again the raw ache that visited her at such moments.

"Ah, James," she said softly, "how I miss you still." Almost a year had passed since she'd laid him to rest. Didn't seem possible. Yet at times she could not envision his face unless she was actually looking at the portrait.

Those times troubled her, as if she were betraying him by allowing the memories of him to fade slowly. Yet in her heart she knew that James would understand. Although the wounds were beginning to heal, that didn't mean she loved him less, or that she no longer treasured the time she had spent with him.

A tap on the door disturbed her thoughts, and she called out, "Come in."

Baxter entered, his expression solemn. "You wished to speak to me, madam?"

"Yes." Cecily sat on her usual chair at the head of the table. "Sit down, Baxter, I want to discuss this puzzle of the two dead men."

"I prefer to stand, thank you, madam."

She frowned up at him. "Do you have any idea how frustrating it is to always be looking up at you when I'm talking to you? Just once I would like to have a conversation with you at eye level."

"Yes, madam." He stayed where he was, his back to the door, his hands behind him.

"I really don't know which is worse, to be treated with disdain by misguided gentlemen who regard women as inferior beings, or to be held at a respectable distance by someone I consider a friend."

Baxter stretched his neck, which was turning red above his stiff white collar. "I did not invent the rules of etiquette, madam. I only follow them."

"Piffle." Cecily let out her breath in a disgusted sigh. She was being unreasonable, and she knew it. But sometimes she wished she could abolish the rules and start all over again with new ones. True, things had improved slightly for women since the Queen's death, but not fast enough. Not nearly fast enough.

"Well, then, please may I have a cigar? At least you can allow me that small triumph over the dark ages?"

She waited patiently through Baxter's pained and laborious performance of handing her a cigar and lighting it for her, then settled back in a cloud of fragrant smoke.

"I am quite worried about these deaths, Baxter. I'm very much afraid that Madeline might find herself in a compromising position. I understand she had been keeping company with both men. That does not put her in a very good light, to say the least."

"It is most unfortunate, I agree. I understand there are rumors in the village about her possible connection with the deaths."

Cecily shook her head. "I still don't see how anything can be proved against her. Dozens of people must have larkspur growing in their gardens."

"Larkspur?" Baxter repeated in surprise.

"Yes, that is what Dr. McDuff believes caused the poisonings."

"Ah," Baxter said, giving her one of his glacier looks. "And he just happened to tell you that, I assume."

Cecily tapped the ring of ash from the end of her cigar into the ashtray. "I went to see him on the pretext of needing a tonic. I needed to know what he had discovered if I'm to help Madeline."

"If Miss Pengrath is guilty, madam, there is nothing you can do to help her."

"Am I the only one, Baxter, who believes Madeline is innocent? Is she to be condemned out of hand simply because she is different? Why is it that we are so ready to believe the worst of someone who does not conform to what we consider to be normal?"

Baxter ran a finger around his collar. "I am not suggesting that Miss Pengrath is responsible for what happened, madam. That is for the police to decide. I merely wish to caution you against becoming involved in something that could cause you a great deal of trouble."

"I appreciate your concern for my well-being." Cecily drew fiercely on the cigar and puffed out the smoke. "I happen to believe that Madeline had nothing to do with these deaths, however, and I intend to prove it."

"May I ask, madam, how you propose to go about doing that?"

"You may, Baxter, and I shall be happy to tell you." Again she flicked a thick slice of ash into the ashtray. "I shall attempt to ferret out the real culprit, of course."

"That is exactly what I am afraid of," Baxter said in a grim tone. "May I remind you, madam, that the last time you interfered in police business, Inspector Cranshaw made it quite clear that he would not tolerate such behavior again."

"You can remind me all you like. I remember it well. But nothing infuriates me more than false assumptions based on ignorance. As you know, the inspector will no doubt rely on Police Constable Northcott to conduct inquiries."

"Heaven help us all," Baxter murmured.

"Exactly." Cecily was well aware of Baxter's dislike of the police constable, though she had never learned the reason for it. It certainly didn't hurt her case to mention his name. "So you can see, we need to be in full control of the facts, if we are to see justice done in this case."

"I cannot condone any action that could cause you trouble with the police," Baxter said stubbornly.

Cecily took a final pull on her cigar and stubbed it out. "Baxter, you might have promised my husband to take care of me, but that does not give you the right to dictate to me my course of action in any given situation. If you care to offer your assistance, however, as a way of honoring your promise to James, I would be most obliged."

She watched frustration cross his face as he struggled with his convictions. Several seconds ticked by, marked by the massive clock on the mantelpiece above the marble fireplace.

Finally Baxter let out his breath in a deep sigh. "I will do my best to assist you, madam. But I cannot promise I will do so without comment or caution, and I wish to state emphatically that I do so with grave misgivings."

"Don't worry, Baxter," Cecily said with great satisfaction. "With you by my side, what could possibly happen?"

Cecily went down to the kitchen later to collect the tablecloths, and found Mrs. Chubb trying to console Gertie, who sat in a chair looking as though the end of the world were imminent.

While Mrs. Chubb went to fetch the linen from her sitting room, Cecily studied the housemaid with concern. "Are you not feeling well?" she asked.

Gertie sprang to her feet and started industriously polishing the silver utensils that were piled on the table. "Oh, I'm all right, thank you, mum. It's Ian I'm worried about." She gave a mournful sigh. "He went up to the lighthouse project to collect his wages what was owed him, and they were downright nasty to him."

"Nasty? In what way?"

"They think he had something to do with the damage what was done up there." Gertie flashed a defiant look at Cecily. "As if he would. He was making good money up there. He'd never do nothing like that, not my Ian wouldn't."

Mystified by this latest revelation, Cecily frowned. "Why do they think Ian had anything to do with it?"

"Because he's the only local on the project, ain't he. Some of the bleeding farmers have been complaining about the lighthouse. They say it's going to hurt the land. And if it's built it will bring bigger ships into Wellercombe, and more food from them foreign lands, so the farms won't sell so much."

This was news to Cecily, who until then had thought that the majority of people in Badgers End were happy about the project. "But what does that have to do with Ian?" she asked, still puzzled.

Gertie laid down a newly polished fork and picked up another. She examined it, spit on it, then began rubbing it with her cloth.

Cecily winced, but said nothing. She would have a quiet word with Mrs. Chubb later, she promised herself. It was the housekeeper's job to chastise the housemaids, and Cecily wasn't about to interfere.

"Well, everyone knows he's a friend of Dick Scroggins, and Dick hates the lighthouse project. They think that Ian only went to work there so he could do the damage and put them off building it." Gertie rubbed furiously on the fork. "Bloody daft, they are," she muttered.

"Well, I'm sure they'll find out sooner or later who sabotaged the project," Cecily said as Mrs. Chubb came bustling back into the kitchen carrying the tablecloths. "That should stop the tongues wagging."

"Well, that ain't the half of it," Gertie said, starting on another fork. "They say Ian could be the one what poisoned those two men, as well. It's all to stop the project, they said." She chewed on her lower lip while she studied the fork. "I know he wouldn't do nothing like that. He's not bloody perfect by any means, but he's no blinking murderer, that I do know."

"Now that's enough, Gertie," Mrs. Chubb put in hurriedly. "You don't need to be bothering madam with all your problems." She handed the tablecloths to Cecily with a smile of apology. "Gets carried away, she does, if I'm not here to stop her."

"Madam asked me," Gertie said in an injured tone. "I was just telling her what she asked, that's all."

"It's all right, Mrs. Chubb," Cecily said, tucking the tablecloths under her arm. "I still consider Ian an employee of mine, and naturally I'm concerned about him."

"Yeah, well, it didn't bloody help him to be fighting with Colin Bickley the night he died, did it?" Gertie said gloomily.

Cecily looked at her with a start. She'd quite forgotten about Ian's fight with Bickley. "Do you know what the fight was about?"

Gertie's face turned a deep shade of red, but she shook her head. "No, I don't," she mumbled, leaving Cecily quite certain the girl was keeping something back.

Making up her mind to have a word with Ian at the earliest opportunity, Cecily left the kitchen. It appeared that there were now two suspects in the case, neither of whom were capable of such a crime, in Cecily's opinion. It would seem that she would have her work cut out for her, unless the police unearthed some new evidence on the case.

What really worried her was the fact that two men had already died, by the same means. Something told her that unless the puzzle could be solved quickly, and whoever was responsible apprehended, it was entirely possible that there could be more deaths in Badgers End.

And heaven alone knew who would be next.

CHAPTER

❖ 10 ❖

Early the next morning Mrs. Chubb huffed and puffed as she climbed the steep slope to Madeline's cottage. The things she did for that girl, she thought, when she finally reached the wooden gate, and leaned on it to get her breath. Must be mad, that's what.

Although she'd never admit it, Mrs. Chubb was very fond of Gertie. She tried to tell herself that it was because she was a good worker, and good workers were hard to find, never mind all the training it took to get them to the point where she didn't have to follow them around all the time.

The truth was, ever since she'd first set eyes on Gertie, twelve years old and eyes big as saucers, her straight black hair falling all over her face, she'd taken the child right to her heart.

Mrs. Chubb had never had children of her own. She lost three of them trying to give birth, and after that the doctors told her she'd never have any more. Gertie was the daughter Mrs. Chubb had always envisioned in her imagination.

The housekeeper straightened her back and pushed open the gate. She hoped from the bottom of her heart that Gertie wasn't pregnant, especially if that loud-mouthed Ian Rossiter was the father. Oh, he had plenty of charm, all right, but he was no good for Gertie. She deserved a lot better than the likes of him.

Mrs. Chubb trudged up the gravel path, between thick rows of gold and crimson chrysanthemums. All she hoped was that something else had made the girl late. And if one of Madeline's potions could bring her on, then both she and Mrs. Chubb could stop worrying about it.

God knows she had enough to worry about without that. And it was upsetting to see Gertie mooching around looking as if she had the troubles of the world on her shoulders. Took her twice as long to get anything done these days.

Mrs. Chubb lifted the brass door knocker with the tip of a gloved finger. The knocker was in the shape of a gargoyle's head. The ugliest thing Mrs. Chubb ever did see. She didn't even like touching it.

The door opened, and Madeline's pretty face appeared in the gap, her hair floating around her head like spray from a waterfall. It had always amazed Mrs. Chubb how hair could float like that. Hers had always lain flat and heavy on her head, which is why she'd always wound it into a bun. She could keep it tidy, if she stuck enough pins in it to hold it.

"Altheda! How nice to see you." Madeline waved a languid hand at her. "I was just making some tea. You're just in time to join me."

"What kind of tea is it?" Mrs. Chubb asked suspiciously as she stepped down into the cluttered front room. Madeline made a living from selling a variety of hand-crafted items, and her entire cottage was her workshop.

At first glance, the room looked like something out of *A Thousand and One Nights*. Folds of material were draped around the walls, soft, smooth, richly hued velvets and pale, filmy gauze. Strings of brightly colored beads hung between the doorways, interlaced with silver and gold ribbons.

An old-fashioned oil lamp dangled from the ceiling. Mrs. Chubb half expected to see smoke pouring from the spout in the shape of a genie. Not that she'd mind having three wishes granted, mind you.

On the sideboard and scattered over the floor lay huge flowers made out of paper in every color of the rainbow, while little furry stuffed animals of every description grinned at her from the corners of the room.

But it was the smell of the place that always disturbed Mrs. Chubb—pungent and spicy, not altogether unpleasant, but strange. Different. Exotic. Foreign. Like those pictures she saw in the lurid magazines that Gertie hid in her bedroom.

"It's chamomile," Madeline said, rattling cups in the kitchen. "Find a place to sit down, and I'll bring you some biscuits."

Mrs. Chubb moved a sewing basket off the seat of an overstuffed armchair and plunked down onto it. It was the most comfortable seat in Madeline's home. Actually it was the only comfortable seat in Madeline's home.

She eyed the steaming cup that Madeline handed her with a wary eye. She had drunk many a cup of strange-tasting tea in that cottage and survived them all, but one never knew what one was drinking.

"I'm surprised to see you," Madeline said as she settled herself on a large velvet cushion in the middle of the floor. "Did you change your day off?"

"No, I didn't." Mrs. Chubb took a cautious sip of the tea. It had a slightly bitter flavor, but was drinkable—though she would have much preferred some strong black Assam. "I came up here to buy a potion," she said, trying to look as if it were the most normal thing in the world to be asking.

Madeline looked at her in astonishment. "Why, Altheda, you gave me to understand you would never touch one of my remedies. That's what doctors are for, I believe you said."

Mrs. Chubb nodded, hoping her face wasn't turning as red as it felt. "Yes, well, it isn't for me, you see. It's for . . . a friend of mine."

Madeline's dark eyes glistened with amusement. "You have a lover, Altheda? Is that it? You want a love potion to make him look at you as he would a young nubile wood nymph?"

A spray of tea spewed from Mrs. Chubb's shocked lips, drenching her skirt. Choking, she tried frantically to hunt in her sleeve for her handkerchief, while balancing the cup and saucer in the other hand.

Madeline casually reached for a beautiful piece of embroidered linen. "Here," she said, offering it to Mrs. Chubb, "use this."

The housekeeper shook her head. "Oh, I couldn't," she croaked.

"Yes, you can." Climbing onto her knees, Madeline dropped the cloth into Mrs. Chubb's lap and then settled back on her cushion. "Now, tell me why you need a potion."

Dabbing at her skirt with the exquisite piece of fabric, Mrs. Chubb tried to find the right words. This was proving to be considerably more difficult than she'd realized.

"I . . . er . . . that is . . . I need a potion to . . . er . . . you know . . . make someone come on."

Madeline looked puzzled. "Come on where?"

Mrs. Chubb tried again. "You know. It. The curse. She's late, you see, and she's scared to death she's in the family way."

Madeline's perfectly shaped eyebrows lifted. "Altheda Chubb! Whatever have you been up to?"

"Not me!" Mrs. Chubb yelped, then succumbed to a fit of coughing.

Madeline scrambled to her feet, took the cup from the housekeeper's jerking hand, and thumped her broad back. "There," she said when the housekeeper gasped in protest, "feeling better?"

Mrs. Chubb nodded frantically, before she could receive another one of those dreadful blows. Almost jerked her off the chair, it did. Madeline sank back onto her cushion and waited for her to get her breath.

"Now," Madeline said, when the sound of rasping breathing had ceased, "start at the beginning and tell me who it is who needs this remedy."

"I promised I wouldn't," Mrs. Chubb said hoarsely. She took the cup Madeline thrust at her and took a hefty gulp of the tea, almost choking again in her attempt to swallow it.

"I can't give it to you unless I know who it's for." Madeline said. "It makes a difference in the mixture, you must realize that."

Mrs. Chubb wasn't at all sure that Madeline wasn't merely being curious, but she'd had enough. Her skirt was damp, her throat felt as if it were on fire, and the embarrassment of the whole situation was just too much to bear. If she'd known getting a potion would be this much trouble, she'd have tried the gin again.

"It's for Gertie," she whispered, though there was no one there except Madeline to hear her. "She's terrified she might be . . ." She practically mouthed the word "pregnant."

Madeline smiled. "Just sit there, and I'll soon mix something up for her."

Mrs. Chubb looked at her anxiously. "It won't . . . hurt it . . . if it is there . . . I don't want that—"

"Don't worry," Madeline said, "all it will do is bring her on. If she is pregnant, then Mother Nature will take care of it, and Gertie will have to prepare to be a mother herself."

Mrs. Chubb fanned her face with the linen cloth. Heaven help the poor child if she was. Then again, having a baby around wouldn't be all that bad. Maybe they could work something out with madam . . . Feeling a little better, Mrs. Chubb waited for the potion.

Cecily had cornered Ian first thing that morning. She'd gone into one of the suites to decide which furnishings should be removed before the chimney sweeps arrived, and found Ian painting the windows.

"Hope this is the right shade, mum," Ian said, standing back to view his work. "They told me at the ironmonger's that it was, but it looks darker to me."

"Don't worry, Ian. The sun will soon bleach it out. That's the problem with blue, it fades so quickly, but it does look nice with the white walls."

Ian looked relieved. "I didn't want to have to do it all again. I just hope the rain keeps off, so I can get this one finished."

Unable to think of a tactful way to broach the subject, Cecily decided to come straight to the point. "Ian, I understand you had a fight with Colin Bickley the night he died."

He sent her a startled look, his paintbrush poised in midair. "Yes, mum, I did. He was asking for it, right enough."

"Something quite drastic must have happened for you to resort to hitting the man. By the looks of your eye, you didn't have it all your way."

He looked at her steadily for several seconds, and she thought he wasn't going to answer her. Then he said softly, "I didn't poison him, Mrs. Sinclair. I wouldn't do that. I know I got a bit of a hot temper, but no matter how bad he upset me, I would never have killed him. I swear on me mother's grave, I didn't do it."

"I wasn't suggesting that you did." She sat down on a green velvet armchair and sank against its tufted back. "I was merely wondering what he had done to provoke that temper of yours."

Ian dropped his gaze to the paintbrush in his hand. "He was pestering Gertie, that's what. We was all in the George the night before. I was practicing me darts, and it was Gertie's night off so she came down to watch me."

Stooping down, he laid the brush on top of the paint pot. "Anyway, while I was at the dart board, Bickley was trying to touch up Gertie, if you'll excuse the expression, mum."

Cecily's lips twitched, but she said nothing.

"Well, Gertie didn't tell me till after we were on the way home. She was afraid I'd lose me temper, like. I might have let it go at that, but Gertie said Bickley told her he wasn't giving up, and he'd have her sooner or later." He straightened, wiping his hands on his overalls. "Well, that made me bloody furious. I couldn't say anything to him at work because he was my boss, and I didn't want to get the sack. So when I went down to the George for my darts practice the next night, I told him to keep his bloody hands off my girl."

"I see. And he didn't like that, I suppose."

"Too right, he didn't. Blew his blinking top. Told me he could have any woman he wanted, and Gertie wasn't my property. It wouldn't have been so bad if I hadn't known what Bickley was like."

Ian made a sound of disgust in the back of his throat. "I don't want to speak ill of the dead, Mrs. Sinclair, but he was the worst kind. Always after the women, he was. Thought he was the blooming answer to their prayers. He got what he could out of them, then dumped 'em. I know, 'cause I heard him bragging about it at work. Bloody proud of it, he was, like he'd done something wonderful."

"So you hit him."

Ian shrugged. "I wanted to let him know what would happen to him if he didn't leave Gertie alone. I told him I'd round up the boys and give him more bother than he could handle. It took a while to put him down, but I did it."

"Did anyone else see the fight?"

"Not only saw it, they all bloody joined in, didn't they. Until Dick threw 'em all out. He was going on about the lighthouse project. Said as how he was going to have a protest march against it."

Cecily shook her head. "I'm amazed how shortsighted some people can be. The lighthouse can bring a lot of benefits to Badgers End. I don't understand why so many people are against it."

"Well, it's all right for the fishermen, I suppose, and the

sailors on the cargo ships, but not everyone likes changes, do they? Some people are afraid of changes, whether they're good or bad. They're happy the way things are, 'cause that's the way it's always been, and that's what they're used to."

Somewhat surprised by his insight, Cecily got up from the chair. "I'm beginning to find that out," she said with a sigh. "But I would suggest in future, Ian, that you try to use more control over your temper. It could get you into a great deal of trouble, if it hasn't already."

"Yes, mum, I know. Gertie said the same thing. I will try. Honest."

"I'm glad to hear it." She swept a glance around the room, noting the items she wanted removed. Then, as she reached the door, she turned back to look at Ian. "Tell me, did Mr. Donaldson join in that fight?"

Looking surprised, Ian shrugged. "Could have done, I suppose. He was down there. I was too busy with Bickley to notice, tell the truth."

"Did the two men spend much time together after work?"

Ian's expression changed to wariness. "I wouldn't know, mum. I never kept company with them, so I don't know what they did, except for when they was drinking down the George. And all the chaps sit together, like, so it would be hard to tell."

"I see," Cecily said. "Well, not to worry." She opened the door and left him alone to finish his painting.

"You've got to drink half of this tonight and the other half tomorrow night," Mrs. Chubb said, handing a bottle of green liquid to Gertie. "Madeline says it should do the trick, all right."

Standing in the middle of Mrs. Chubb's sitting room, Gertie held up the bottle and peered at it. "What if it doesn't?"

"Then it'll be time to tell Ian Rossiter that he's going to be a father, and he'd better do something about making an honest woman of you."

Gertie made a face. "I don't know as I want to be married to the likes of him."

"You won't have much choice if you are pregnant," Mrs. Chubb said, feeling irritated with the girl. In her opinion, Gertie should have thought about all that before letting a man have his way with her.

There was enough written about the subject lately, how women could protect themselves from getting pregnant. In fact, she was quite sure Gertie must have read about it in those dreadful magazines she had.

Not that Mrs. Chubb approved of such scandalous behavior, of course. Actually she couldn't imagine why any woman would do it unless she had to. Nasty messy business, it was.

"Well, I ain't going to be pregnant after I've taken this stuff," Gertie said, tucking the bottle into the pocket of her apron.

"You hope." Mrs. Chubb looked up at the clock on the mantel. "For heaven's sake, Gertie, look at the time. Mrs. Parmentier will be waiting for her breakfast tray. You're never going to get anything done if you don't get on with it. And tell Ethel to get a move on. I swear that girl gets lazier every day."

"I don't know why the Black Widow can't come down to breakfast like everyone else," Gertie grumbled. "Every meal taken in her room, and it's me what has to trudge up and down those stairs with her trays."

"She's in mourning," Mrs. Chubb said, flinging open the door as a hint to Gertie to get moving. "New widows don't mix with people, and you know it. Now go and tell Michel you're ready to take up the tray."

Gertie shuffled along to the kitchen, her mind on the bottle in her apron pocket. It had to work, she told herself as she pushed open the door. It had to. Much as she loved Ian, she wasn't ready to marry him yet.

She wasn't ready to marry anyone yet. She certainly wasn't ready to have a baby. What did she know about babies? Probably powder the wrong end, knowing her.

Michel's short temper did nothing to soothe her frazzled nerves. The chef had a habit of crashing the pots and pans around when he was in a bad mood, and every sound seemed to split her head open. She was glad when the tray was finally ready and she could escape from the steamy kitchen.

By the time she reached the top of the stairs, she was out of breath. The heavy tray dragged on her shoulder muscles, and her arms ached, her back ached, and her legs ached. She just hoped the Black Widow appreciated the extra work she caused.

Balancing the tray on her knee, Gertie rapped on the door of Mrs. Parmentier's suite. After a long wait, the door opened, slowly and cautiously, and the heavily veiled face slid into view.

"Your breakfast, ma'am," Gertie said, hoisting the tray in the air. "Sorry it's late." Pain sped along her arms and down her back, but she managed to keep a smile fixed firmly on her face.

"That's all right. Thank you," Mrs. Parmentier said. She sounded as if she had a bad cold. The door opened wider, and two large hands took the tray from Gertie's grasp.

Gertie tried valiantly not to think about those hands hauling her naked body out of the bathtub. She hoped the Black Widow wasn't thinking about it, either.

She was about to turn away when the husky voice said, "I trust you are feeling better?"

"Not much," Gertie said without thinking. Then it occurred to her that she should at least sound grateful for the woman's help, even though it embarrassed her that the widow had mentioned the subject. "I appreciate you helping me, ma'am," she said, hoping the widow wouldn't make a big song and dance about it.

"Don't mention it. I was happy to be of assistance."

For a moment Gertie stared at the veiled face, wishing she could see what the woman looked like. Then a strange, creepy feeling crept over her, and she blurted out a hasty "Thank you, ma'am."

Scooting down the landing to the stairs, she could feel the invisible eyes boring into her back, then she heard the door close quietly behind her. Her palms felt damp on the banister rail as she started down the stairs. That was one very strange woman.

CHAPTER

❧ 11 ❧

In the dining room, Cecily finished her light breakfast of kippers and scrambled eggs, and sat sipping fragrant coffee served in a fragile demitasse that was part of the Pennyfoot's elegant bone china tableware.

It was difficult to sit there in the quiet, elegant surroundings and think about the two men who had died so horribly. Yet the events kept playing over in her mind. The entire situation puzzled her a great deal.

She simply could not accept the possibility of either Madeline or Ian being responsible for the poisoning, though she could well understand the inspector's suspicion of foul play. On the face of it, the source of the poison would have to come from the George and Dragon, since both men had died shortly after leaving there.

It didn't seem likely that only two men had died such a swift and violent death, however, when several more had apparently eaten the same food and drank the same beer. Then there was the discrepancy in the time of death. Taking all that into consideration, it seemed unlikely that the deaths could be coincidental.

On the other hand, if the two men had been murdered, that would mean they had been singled out. Which pointed to a connection between them of some sort. Maybe if she could pinpoint that connection, Cecily thought as she refilled her cup with the silver coffee pot, perhaps it would throw some light upon a possible suspect.

Still pondering the problem, she drained the cup and set it down on the saucer. As she did so, she caught sight of Baxter hovering in the doorway.

The second she saw his face, she knew he had brought bad news. Hurrying across the floor toward him, she could only guess at whatever it was he had to tell her.

"The library?" she asked as she reached him.

"If you wish, madam." His gray eyes were full of concern, and Cecily grew even more worried. She had a dreadful feeling she knew what he was about to tell her.

She led the way to the library and shut the door behind them. "It's Madeline, isn't it," she said before he could say a word.

Baxter nodded gravely. "I'm afraid so, madam. The police have taken Miss Pengrath into Wellercombe. They want to question her in connection with the deaths of Bickley and Donaldson."

Phoebe hurried up the steps of the Pennyfoot Hotel, one hand holding on to the wide brim of her dove-gray hat. The stiff breeze had sprung up as she had reached the end of the Esplanade, and unprepared for it, she had neglected to anchor the hat securely enough.

In spite of its weight, it threatened to take flight with each tug of the mischievous wind. Phoebe had visions of it sailing over the railing into the ocean, off to parts unknown.

She was particularly fond of that hat. Dear Sedgely had bought it for her from Marshall and Snelgrove's shortly after their marriage. She had worn it to afternoon tea with the Duchess of Morden and received a very nice compliment from the gracious lady.

Although that was more years ago than she wanted to remember, she still felt that it suited her very well, with its tiny white silk roses and several yards of blue tulle. The white parrot was a nice touch, she had always thought, and looked quite lifelike. She almost expected it to talk.

The thought amused her, and she had a half smile on her face as she walked into the lobby of the hotel. She heard her name called almost immediately and, caught unawares, had turned in response to it before she had time to think twice.

She saw Mr. Baxter heading toward her, a look of grim determination on his face. To her intense consternation, that dreadful artist fellow trailed right behind him.

Feeling a distinct fluttering in the region of her heart, Phoebe hoped she would not faint. There seemed no escape now as the two men bore down on her. Taking a tight hold of her parasol just in case she should need it, she waited with bated breath.

"Mrs. Carter-Holmes," Mr. Baxter announced to anyone within earshot, "I am so glad to see you. Mr. Rawlins has been begging to make your acquaintance, and I promised him an introduction. It was just by chance we happened to be in the lobby when you arrived."

Really, Phoebe thought, eying the fragile figure of the artist with a mixture of distaste and suspicion. More like the despicable man was lying in wait for her. There was nothing for it but to condescend to an introduction. If she refused now, she would appear lacking in etiquette, a flaw that Phoebe would never allow.

As she had suspected, Sidney Rawlins looked to be in his early forties. Somewhat younger than her, in any case. His light blond hair hung far too low below his shoulders, and his shaggy beard hadn't seen the blades of scissors since it was conceived.

As for his clothes . . . quite, quite dreadful. With that

shapeless velvet jacket and ill-fitting trousers, he looked as if he'd been dressed from the rag bag.

"Mrs. Carter-Holmes," Mr. Baxter said in his pompous voice, "may I present to you Mr. Sidney Rawlins, celebrated artist of some renown and connoisseur of fine art."

Doing her best to hide her revulsion, Phoebe offered her gloved fingertips. To her surprise, the artist took them and touched them gently with his lips. She was even more surprised when he spoke.

"Madam," he said in an exquisite voice, "I am so honored to make your acquaintance."

She was almost disarmed by that mellow tone, until she looked into his eyes. Dark brown, they were, and seemed to burn with a strange, fierce light. As she stared at them, she felt as if she were being drawn down a long, long passageway, faster and faster, helpless to stop as the walls rushed past her.

Her heart began pounding, and to her horror she felt drops of perspiration forming on her upper lip. The indignity of it jerked her out of her momentary trance. She snatched her hand back as if it had touched a steaming caldron.

"Mr. Rawlins," she murmured breathlessly, flashing a beseeching look at Mr. Baxter, whose face bore no expression whatsoever.

"Mrs. Carter-Holmes," Sidney Rawlins said in what could only be called bell-like tones, "I have an important matter I wish to discuss with you. I wonder if we could find a secluded corner where we might talk?"

Reluctant to stare into those mesmerizing eyes again, Phoebe stared at his beard in shocked outrage. A secluded corner? What did the man think she was, for heaven's sake? A common street hussy in need of excitement? Looking directly at Mr. Baxter, and ignoring his companion, she said as haughtily as she could manage, "If you will excuse me, Mr. Rawlins, Mr. Baxter, I have urgent business to discuss with Mrs. Sinclair. I was on my way to her suite when you . . . waylaid me."

She liked the sound of that word. It sounded discreet, yet

smacked of her disapproval at being subjected to speaking with such an odd, disreputable character. Hoping that Mr. Baxter understood her message, she swept around and with a rustle of silk headed quickly for the stairs.

Behind her, she heard Mr. Rawlins say urgently, "But, madam, I assure you—"

She wasn't sure what the horrible man was assuring her of, since his words were cut off, presumably by Mr. Baxter's warning hand. Thankful that she hadn't had to deal with the problem by herself, Phoebe climbed the stairs a great deal faster than she was used to doing.

She was quite breathless when she reached the door of Cecily's suite, though whether from exertion or aggravation she wasn't quite sure.

Cecily viewed Phoebe's flushed face with a certain amount of concern. In her opinion, Phoebe always wore her clothes too tight, not so much in the interest of fashion, which was beginning to advocate the looser corset, but in an attempt to preserve her tiny waist.

Under the royal-blue cloak that Phoebe wore, her full breasts rose up and down like a pair of bellows, and her hand fluttered incessantly in front of her face as she tried in vain to fan away the heat.

"My dear," Cecily said in some alarm, "whatever has provoked you into such a state?"

"In a moment," Phoebe puffed, staggering toward a chair. She plopped down on it far too hard to be genteel, and Cecily raised her eyebrows. This wasn't like Phoebe at all.

She sat herself down on a dark red velvet chair and waited for her friend to catch her breath. After a while, when Phoebe continued to pant and wheeze, Cecily said tentatively, "Perhaps if you loosened your corset?"

Phoebe's breath refueled in a rush. "This has nothing to do with my attire," she said tersely. "In any case, I never loosen my corset until I retire to my bed. A woman can lose her figure so quickly once she starts to let herself go."

Cecily didn't say so, of course, but she knew what the remark implied. Phoebe had never approved of Cecily's habit of doing without a corset. In Phoebe's eyes, that was sacrilege to the attributes the Good Lord had seen fit to bestow on women in general and Phoebe Carter-Holmes in particular.

Refusing to let the words rankle, Cecily said mildly, "As you wish. But I would like to know what has upset you to the point of seizure."

"That dreadful creature, that's what . . . who," Phoebe said, clutching her still-heaving breast. "Can you imagine, the brute actually wanted to get me into a dark corner somewhere. With Mr. Baxter standing right there, if you please. Thank heavens he was there. If not, I dread to think what would have become of me. I can't imagine what he was thinking of, introducing a lady of my background to that despicable degenerate."

A glimmer of understanding penetrated the fog. Cecily smiled. "Baxter introduced you to Sidney Rawlins?"

"He most certainly did. I can't imagine why. All the man wanted was to get me off somewhere so he can have his way with me."

Cecily had a great deal of trouble keeping her face straight. "Are you quite sure of his intentions? I really don't think—"

"Ah, that's the trouble, you see. It would seem that neither you nor Mr. Baxter have given this much thought. You both seem to have been taken in by this creature. You only have to look at the man to see what he is. Those terrible eyes, all that hair, those dreadful clothes . . ." Phoebe shook her head as if words failed her.

Cecily was about to reply when Phoebe leaned forward and said in a hoarse whisper, "He doesn't even trim his beard. Can you imagine? He probably hasn't bathed in months."

"I think I would know if that were true," Cecily said, promising herself she would have a stern word with Baxter for ignoring her advice.

"Well, I must say, this entire episode has left my nerves

in a most delicate state. What with this and the news about Madeline—"

"News? Have you heard anything new?"

Phoebe looked taken aback by Cecily's concern. "Only that Inspector Cranshaw has asked her to go to Wellercombe to answer some questions. 'Helping them with their inquiries,' was the phrase I heard. Most likely advising them on poisonous plants, I should think."

News traveled fast, Cecily thought, deciding not to worry Phoebe with her own fears. "Yes, I'm sure that's it."

"I don't know about you," Phoebe said, reaching into her handbag for a handkerchief, "but I could do with a strong cup of tea and one of Dolly's pastries. Would you care to accompany me? I do believe it's my turn to treat."

They could just as easily have afternoon tea in the hotel, Cecily thought. But she felt depressed over the plight of her friend and her own inability to help her. Perhaps a breath of fresh air would do her good.

"I'll be happy to join you," she said, getting to her feet. "Give me a moment to freshen my face." Leaving Phoebe alone, she crossed the room to her boudoir and closed the door behind her.

Dolly's Tea Shop had few customers when Cecily and Phoebe arrived there later. Louise graciously seated them, then left them alone to chat while she went to prepare their tray.

For once, Phoebe had nothing to say about the quiet-spoken assistant. After mulling aloud over her choice of pastries, she sat back in her chair with a sigh of relief.

"This is so pleasant just sitting here and relaxing," she said, smoothing each glove up her arm. "Such a nice refined atmosphere. I really don't know what we would do without the tea shop. It's a haven away from all the turmoil going on outside. So safe and cozy."

Watching the flames in the huge fireplace leap for the chimney, Cecily felt inclined to agree with her friend. In the first few months after James had died, she had been most reluctant to leave the hotel. Finally she had allowed Phoebe to persuade her to return to the tea shop, and after her long absence, Cecily had felt as though she had returned to the home of dear friends.

It was almost as familiar to her as her own home had been, before she'd been forced to sell it and move into the Pennyfoot. The china jugs and vases on the wide mantelpiece, the decorative plates balanced on the picture rail, the large copper coal scuttle standing in the hearth, and the polished brass fender with the dent in the right-hand corner were all implanted in her memory since she had been a small child kneeling on a chair to reach the table.

She started as a strident voice declared, "I'm happy to see some people are not scared off by the goings-on in the village."

Looking up into Dolly's florid face, Cecily said quietly, "I do hope these incidents haven't had an effect on your business."

Dolly's fleshy shoulders lifted in a shrug. "Aye, there's always some as frighten easily. I'll be glad when they catch whoever done it, that's for sure. All this talk of poisoning, people'll be afraid to eat anything. It could close me down, that's what."

"Well, it seems as if you might lose quite a few of your customers, anyway," Phoebe said as Louise arrived with the loaded tray and set it on the table. "There's talk of the workmen returning to London now that work has stopped on the lighthouse. They say it could be some time before the equipment can be replaced."

Louise made a tutting noise. "We won't miss them nearly as much as the George and Dragon will. That's where they spend all their money. If you ask me, the owner should be grateful for all that extra business, instead of complaining all the time. He's done nothing but stir up trouble ever since I've been there. I'll be glad when I can move into the cottage. All that brawling and carrying on is most disconcerting."

Dolly nodded. "It can get on your nerves, duck, when

you're not used to that sort of behavior. You'll be a lot better off when you're in that cottage." She slapped her hands on her ample hips, sending a cloud of flour into the air. "Well, I can't stand here gossiping all day. If I don't make some more pastries, I'll be losing what customers I've got left."

With a cheery wave of her hand she stomped back to the kitchen, leaving Louise to serve the tea.

"When will you be moving into the cottage?" Cecily asked, watching the steady stream of brown liquid pour into her cup.

"At the end of the month, I'm told," Louise answered. She set the teapot back on its stand. "It can't be soon enough for me."

"Have you looked at the cottage?" Cecily asked, reaching for her cup.

Louise nodded. "I went over it very thoroughly, I can tell you. I'm fussy about where I live."

"I take it there wasn't a need for repairs, then?"

The assistant looked at her, clearly puzzled. "Repairs? Not at all."

Cecily sipped the tea, then set her cup down. "I merely wondered, that's all. I seem to have heard somewhere that there was a possibility of someone breaking into the cottage the night that Mr. Bickley died."

Louise looked shocked. "Oh, my, no. I'm quite sure of that. All the windows and doors have heavy locks and bolts, and nothing was broken, or I would surely have seen it."

"Does it concern you," Phoebe said, "inhabiting a cottage where a man has so recently died?"

"Not at all." Louise plopped two lumps of sugar into Phoebe's cup. "The man has no doubt paid for his sins. I have to atone only for mine. As we all do."

For a moment Phoebe looked taken aback by this statement. "I'm sure that's a comforting thought," she murmured.

"I can assure you I shall enjoy the peace and quiet of Hawthorne Lane, after the ruckus I've had to put up with."

"It must be dreadful," Phoebe said, narrowing her eyes.

"So distressing to have to put up with such ribald revelry. I'm quite sure you're used to more refined surroundings."

She waited hopefully, smiling up at Louise's face in encouragement. Her disappointment was evident in her expression when Louise merely nodded. "Will there be anything else, Mrs. Sinclair?"

"Thank you, but I believe we have sufficient for now," Cecily said, placing her serviette on her lap.

Louise backed away and returned to the counter, where a large burly man stood waiting to be served.

Phoebe shook her head. "I really do feel so sorry for the woman," she said in a low voice. "Must be absolutely dreadful for her."

Cecily agreed, then deliberately changed the subject. She had far more urgent problems on her mind than the plight of Louise Atkins.

CHAPTER

❋12❋

Cecily's anxiety increased considerably when she returned
to the hotel. Shortly after she'd arrived in her suite, Gertie
tapped on her door with a message from Baxter, requesting
a meeting with her in the library.

He was waiting for her when she walked in there several
minutes later. She knew at once he had bad news.

"I'm sorry, madam," he said as he sat down at the end of
the table, "but I have just received a message from Wellercombe. It seems that Inspector Cranshaw has seen fit to
detain Miss Pengrath overnight. There is no word as to
when or if she will be released."

"I see." She had feared as much. Cecily stared up at the
portrait of James, hoping to gain strength from his beloved
image. "We will have to get in touch with my solicitor in the
morning. Will you please have a message sent to him first
thing?"

"Of course, madam. I have already taken the liberty of informing Messrs. Thompson, Thompson and Croft of the circumstances, and the possibility that you might wish to obtain their services in this matter."

"Thank you, Baxter." She smiled. "What would I do without you?"

Baxter cleared his throat and stretched his neck. "I would hope, madam, that at least in the near future you will not be in the position of doing without me."

"So would I, Bax," Cecily said softly, "so would I."

Taking pity on his discomfort, she changed the subject. "I find this entire situation a puzzle. Two men dead, with the same symptoms, apparently from the same cause. Except for one interesting fact. The time it took them to die. I'm afraid that is the one factor that makes things look so black for Madeline."

Baxter rocked back and forth on his heels, his hands clasped behind his back. "I wonder if perhaps Bickley took something home with him from the pub to eat later?"

Cecily shook her head. "According to Ian, there were several witnesses who swore that Colin Bickley ate nothing at the George and Dragon. After he ate at Madeline's, he wasn't hungry. And if he took something home from Madeline's, then we are back to suspicion being pointed at her."

"It could have been an accident," Baxter said gently.

"Twice? I doubt it. And the police certainly would question such a coincidence. No, I have to believe the poison was in the beer. But if so, why was only one man affected by it, and the next night, one more?"

"It would certainly appear that someone deliberately poisoned the beer."

"Undoubtedly." Cecily sighed. "But then, according to Dr. McDuff, death is instant in this type of poisoning. So how is it that Colin Bickley was able to walk for half an hour, with no visible signs of distress, and then die several minutes later after he'd arrived home?"

"He must have ingested the poison inside his own home."

"Perhaps. But that would mean someone would have to break into the cottage and place the poison there."

Baxter's eyebrows lifted. "I wonder if the police have considered this theory."

"Most likely not, if it was left to Northcott. Not that it matters. Louise Atkins has assured me there was no sign of a break-in at the cottage when she inspected it." She rose, signaling the end of the discussion. "It's unfortunate that Dr. McDuff can be so specific about the cause of poisoning. Had it not been for the diagnosis of larkspur as the culprit, the police might not have been so ready to accuse Madeline."

"The doctor is certain of his conclusion?"

Cecily nodded. "Apparently the blue tinge to the skin of the victims confirmed it." She frowned as a picture popped into her mind—a vision of Colonel Fortescue, waxed mustache quivering with excitement as he related one of his bizarre tales.

Something he said . . . ah, she had it now. She remembered quite clearly. *Reminds me of the time I saw a chap turn blue. Went down like a felled elephant. Died right where he stood, they said. One minute he was chipper, the next he was writhing on the ground.*

"Excuse me, Baxter," she said, heading for the door, "but I need to find Colonel Fortescue. For once I want to listen to one of his stories."

An unusual silence prevailed in the public bar of the George and Dragon as Ian stood poised, a dart balanced expertly between his thumb and first two fingers. He needed a double top to finish. Double twenty to win the game.

Surrounded by several workmen, all with a foaming pint mug clutched in their fists, Ian narrowed his eyes. The tiny strip on the outside edge of the circle looked very thin. But he knew he could do it. It was all in the wrist.

He was a bit nervous now. His first throw had gone wide. He'd aimed a little high, afraid of landing the dart on an odd number and messing up the score. Now he was down to two chances. Just two darts. He lowered his hand a fraction, aimed carefully, and with a flick of his wrist let fly.

The dart thudded into the cork, right on the wire. Dick Scroggins stepped up to the board. "It's out," he announced, provoking groans from Ian's teammates and a cheer from his opponent.

Ian felt a twinge of apprehension. All this talk of murder had unsettled his nerves. He needed to concentrate. His fingers smoothed the feathered flights, and he stood for a moment, focusing on the task at hand. Then he drew the familiar aroma of pipe smoke and beer into his nostrils, twitched his nose, blinked his eyes, and took aim again.

Go in, you bugger, he silently ordered, and flicked his hand forward. The dart sailed from his fingers, sure and true, and landed solidly in the middle of the double top space.

"Game," Dick Scroggins announced, and Ian walked up to the board amid cheers to retrieve his darts.

"Right, lads," the portly pub owner said, clapping his hands, "who's next?"

"I'm going to get a drink," Ian said, putting his darts back in their case. "Let someone else have a bash for a while." Pleased with himself, he began pushing his way to the bar through the chattering crowd of laborers. He had almost reached the counter when he saw a man he recognized.

Ian stopped short. The customer was a reporter from London. He'd been down a week or so earlier, doing a story on the lighthouse project. Ian had taken an instant dislike to the man. He'd been pushy, nosy, asking a lot of personal questions that had nothing to do with the job.

Ian didn't like personal questions. His private life was his own business and nobody else's. He definitely didn't want to natter about it to a cocky newsman from the city.

He waited for a moment, hoping the bloke would down his beer and leave. Then, to his intense irritation, he heard the man ask for him by name.

Gerry, the barman, turned his head, his glance sweeping the heads that crowded the room. Ian had no idea why the reporter should want to speak to him again. He didn't want to know. Whatever it was, it was probably trouble. Anything to do with London was trouble for Ian. That's why he'd left.

He moved. Quickly. Before Jerry could spot him. Ducking behind a burly northerner with a thick neck and massive shoulders, Ian slipped through the connecting door into the saloon bar.

He chose a seat in the corner, by the exit door. He could see through the glass if the reporter left the pub. And he was close enough to leave himself if the bloke came looking for him. He ordered a beer and settled down to wait.

Gertie sat at the tiny dressing table in her room and looked at the bottle sitting on the lace doily. The mixture was a thick, slimy green. Gertie didn't want to think what it reminded her of. It was bad enough she had to drink the stuff.

She picked up the bottle and tipped it back and forth, watching a small bubble make its way down to the bottom of the bottle and back up. Half now and half tomorrow night. Then she'd know. If she hadn't seen the curse by then, she'd know for sure that she was pregnant.

"Strewth," Gertie whispered out loud. How the hell was she going to tell Ian he was going to be a father? More important, how would he take it? What would he do? She couldn't bear to think about it. Half of her was scared to death that he'd take off back to London and leave her in the lurch. The other half was just as scared he'd want to marry her.

Gertie didn't want to get married. She'd seen what it did to people. Her own mum and dad drank down the pub till all hours, then threw bloody great saucepans at each other afterward—when they weren't threatening her within an inch of her life, that was.

She'd seen the others, too. Women dragging scruffy, barefooted nippers by the hand, freezing cold with runny noses, shouting and yelling that there'd be no dinner that night if they didn't bring some money home.

No, she was better off with only herself to think about. Gertie looked at her face in the splotched mirror and sighed. Why couldn't women just have fun and enjoy themselves, without worrying about ending up with a bun in the oven?

Why couldn't the bleeding men have the babies instead? Soon put a knot in their whatsit if they did, she was bloody sure of that. They was too bleeding quick to have a bit, that was the problem. It was all right for them, they didn't have to worry about getting lumbered.

She tried not to notice her fingers shaking as she unscrewed the lid of the bottle. She had to concentrate, that was it. If she thought hard enough, it would happen. All she had to do was swallow half of this stuff, then think really, really hard. And in the morning she'd be all right.

Gertie sniffed the mixture gingerly. It smelled like newly mowed grass, with something like peppermint mixed in. Gawd, she thought. She'd never been so flipping anxious to have the curse in her life.

Closing her eyes, she touched the neck of the bottle with her tongue. The taste was sharp, like lemons, yet it wasn't bitter. She tipped her head back, took a mouthful of the stuff, and swallowed.

Ian was halfway through his pint when he finally saw the reporter leave the George by the street door. Taking the pewter mug with him, Ian went back to the public bar and was greeted by a chorus of cheers.

"Thought you'd gone home, mate," one of his fellow workers said, slapping him on the back. "How about taking a few of us on, then? Last one round the clock buys the beer."

Ian grinned. "Sounds all right to me." He could beat every one of these yobs single-handed. It looked like being a good night after all.

Half an hour later he was going for his third win. The crowd had become boisterous, shouting insults and comments louder and louder as the beer flowed.

"Here, me old cod's wallop," one of the players roared, "just watch me sink this dart, then."

Ian recognized the burly laborer he'd hidden behind to escape from the reporter.

"Sink it?" Dick Scroggins let out a belly laugh. "You couldn't sink a paper boat full of holes. Bet you miss by a mile."

"Oh, yeah?" The sturdy man swayed on his feet, but the hand holding the dart looked steady enough. "Well, if you're so frigging sure I'm going to miss, what about if I aim right between your eyes? Let's see how cocky you sound then."

Dick's face turned a dull shade of red. "That's just what I'd expect from one of you ignorant bastards. This isn't the back streets of London, you know. We're a little more civilized than you hooligans. Dragged up through the slums, what else can you expect?"

"Here," the laborer demanded, "who the hell are you calling a bastard?"

Ian, watching from the edge of the circle of onlookers, started backing away. The last thing he wanted was to get mixed up in another fight. His eye was still sore from the last one.

"You, that's who I'm talking to," Dick said belligerently, squaring his shoulders. "I'll be glad when the bloody lot of you have gone back where you belong. You've brought nothing but trouble here, and we're getting sick of it."

"Yeah, well, talking about getting sick, you're frigging lucky to have anyone drink your stinking beer. How many more of us are you going to poison with the stuff, that's what I want to know."

The last thing Ian saw before he slid out of the door was Dick throwing himself at the ugly brute.

Wouldn't give much for the owner's chances, Ian thought, as he hunched his shoulders against the cool night breeze. He shivered and quickened his step. A brisk walk home would put some warmth in his body and make him tired enough to sleep.

He'd gone only a few steps when he saw what looked like a sack of potatoes lying at the side of the road. Someone must have dropped them off his cart on his way home.

The wind caught the gas lamp hanging from the corner of the pub and sent shadows swooping across the road as Ian moved closer to investigate. Maybe it was apples, he thought. He could take some up to the hotel and talk Mrs. Chubb into baking him an apple pie.

Smiling at the thought, he approached the lumpy bundle. The closer he got, the less sure he was that it was a sack. In fact, now that he could see it better, it looked very much like a man lying there.

Shaking his head, Ian walked up to the still figure. The bloke was sprawled on his side, his arms clutched to his body, his face hidden. Stupid twit had probably drunk so much he'd passed out. He'd have one hell of a headache in the morning and serve him bloody well right.

Leaning over the drunk, Ian grabbed a handful of his jacket to turn him over. Might as well see who it was. Probably one of the yobs from the project.

He heaved at the jacket and rolled the man onto his back. As he did so, the wind blew the lamp again, this time sending a shaft of light across the frozen face. The man looked blue with cold.

Ian's heart seemed to lurch in his chest. The face didn't look real. More like a mask. No, it couldn't be. Not another one. But he knew, before he touched the ice-cold skin, that the man was a goner.

Bile rose in his throat as he looked at the distorted face. In the swaying light of the gas lamp, he could see the features quite clearly. It was the man who had been asking for him less than an hour ago. The reporter from London. A very dead reporter.

"Oh, my," Mrs. Chubb said, one hand clutching her throat. "Not another one. Oh, dear Lord, we'll be murdered in our beds at this rate. There's a maniac running around out there. Whatever will we do?"

"We'll let the police take care of it," Ian said, huddling by the roaring stove. "That's their job, ennit?"

"But three." Mrs. Chubb moaned. "What if they don't find the murderer? He could wipe out half the village at this rate."

"I don't think he's after the villagers," Ian said, staring into the blazing coals. "So far all the victims have been from London."

Mrs. Chubb lifted the heavy copper kettle from the stove and carried it over to the sink. "Well, it's only a matter of time before he starts on us. I hope to God the police catch him soon. I'm not going to eat another thing until they do, except what's right here in this kitchen."

Ian shook his head, trying to escape from the dreadful memory of the man's twisted, agonized face. "It might not be a him," he said carefully.

Mrs. Chubb slopped water on the floor as she carried the kettle back to the stove. Dumping it down with a crash, she sent a startled look at Ian. "Whatever do you mean, it's not a him?"

"I heard some of the men talking down the George," Ian said, holding his cold hands out to the oven's steady warmth. "They was talking about Madeline Pengrath."

He heard Mrs. Chubb's hiss of breath and looked up. She stood looking down at him with an outraged expression on her dumpy face.

"People are always talking about Madeline," she said, folding her arms across her chest. "I never take notice of what they say. People are always afraid of what they don't understand."

"Well, maybe they have something to be afraid of this time."

Mrs. Chubb's eyebrows drew together. "Just what the devil are you talking about, Ian Rossiter?"

Pleased with the reaction he was getting to his words, Ian took his time. "Oh, just something I heard down the pub, that's all."

He yawned, and stretched his arms above his head. "I'm

bloody tired, I am. Must be the shock of finding that dead man. I'll never forget what he looked like—"

"Either you tell me what you heard about Madeline this instant," Mrs. Chubb said, leaning over him, "or I'll box your ears."

Ian grinned up at her. "Who you going to get to help you?"

"None of your lip, young man. I'm quite capable of putting you in your place, and you know it. One word from me and Mrs. Sinclair might not be so ready to give you your job back when you want it."

Ian knew when he'd pushed enough. "All right, all right. Give me a mince pie with my tea, and I'll tell you what I heard."

"You're not getting a morsel to eat until you've told me. And make it fast, or you're out on your backside, double quick."

Ian crossed his feet and pushed them closer to the stove. "I heard that Madeline Pengrath has been picked up by the law and taken to Wellercombe for the night."

"No." Mrs. Chubb shook her head in disbelief. "What would they go and do a thing like that for?"

"'Cos they suspect her of poisoning the two blokes, that's why." Ian's stomach heaved as he remembered the reporter. "Looks like it might be three now, with this one."

"Madeline?" Mrs. Chubb made a sound of disgust. "For heaven's sake, where are their brains? Madeline wouldn't hurt a flea. I've never heard of anything so ridiculous in my entire life. Anyone who knows her knows she loves people and animals. Look at all the trouble she goes to making potions to make them well."

"That," said Ian darkly, "is what they think killed the blokes. Madeline Pengrath's potions."

He was looking at the fire and didn't see the housekeeper's expression. But he heard her choked gasp, followed by a shrill shriek. It made him jump.

"Oh, my God," she said in a strange kind of whisper that made his blood run cold. "What have I done?"

He opened his mouth to ask her what she was talking about, but before he could get a word out, she'd turned and stumbled to the door.

"What's wrong?" he asked in alarm, but she was gone, and he could hear the footsteps thudding down the hallway. Shrugging, he sat back in his chair. There were no understanding women. No chance at all. Even Gertie had been acting strange lately, and he couldn't get out of her what the problem was.

Leaning his chin on his hands, he stared into the fire and tried not to think about the twisted body he'd left lying in the road.

Cecily paced in the library, unable to settle down ever since Ian had arrived with the dreadful news. She had sent Baxter in the trap to the George and Dragon right away to find out what he could.

From what she could make out from Ian's somewhat garbled account, the newest victim was a stranger to the village. If he had, in fact, arrived that day, after Madeline had been taken into Wellercombe, that could certainly have an effect on the inspector's case.

His whereabouts would rule out the theory that her potions were the cause of the poisonings.

Cecily sat down at the end of the table. Of course, it wasn't certain yet that the poor man had died from the same thing as the other two. It could be a simple heart attack.

But Ian had been positive the man's skin was blue, and the fact that he had died within several feet of the George and Dragon suggested that the victim had met the same fate as his predecessors. If that was true, then Madeline would almost certainly be cleared of suspicion.

Cecily gazed up at her late husband's portrait. "If you are watching up there, James," she whispered aloud, "say a prayer for Madeline."

CHAPTER

❖ 13 ❖

The door opened abruptly, startling Cecily. For once, Baxter had neglected to knock. He stood in the doorway, his thick hair ruffled by the wind. Smoothing it back with his palm, he stepped into the room.

"Well?" she demanded before he could utter a word. "What did you find out?"

"Not a lot, I'm afraid, madam. The body has been taken into the parlor while they await the arrival of the police. Apparently Police Constable Northcott has handed the case over to Inspector Cranshaw. It will be some time before he arrives at the pub to make his inspection."

"What about Dr. McDuff? Has he determined the cause of death?"

"The doctor is up at the Manor House. I understand Lord Withersgill has a nasty case of the gout, and the doctor is treating him."

Frustrated, Cecily stared at him. "Does no one know when the dead man arrived in Badgers End?"

Baxter shrugged an apology. "Not that I could ascertain, madam."

Pushing back her chair, Cecily stood. "Then, in that case, Baxter, you and I shall go to the George and Dragon, and I will endeavor to find out the facts myself."

As she expected, a look of stubborn disapproval swept across Baxter's face. "Madam, I cannot allow—"

"It is not your business to allow or disallow anything," Cecily reminded him quietly. "I intend to go there, Baxter, with or without you. This might be the only chance we have of clearing Madeline of suspicion. I cannot imagine how distressing all this must be for her, and the sooner we get this cleared up, the better."

"Madam, in all conscience, I cannot—"

"Yes, you can." Cecily stood firm. This was no time to listen to Baxter's objections. That could come later, and probably would. "Order the trap for me at once. I want to be there in time to make my own inquiries before the inspector arrives. If you refuse to accompany me, then I shall go on my own. But I am going. I'm afraid that nothing you can say or do will stop me."

Cecily sat in the trap facing Baxter, her hat held down by a thick mohair stole tied under her chin. Even so, the night air chilled her, or maybe it was nerves, she thought as the steady clop of the bay's hooves disturbed the quiet peace.

The sea mist curled around the gas lamps that lined the Esplanade, forming odd, glowing circles of orange light at the top of the poles. Beyond them the darkness swallowed up the sea, leaving only the soft swish of waves on the cold, hard sand to indicate its presence.

The tiny stores had long been closed for the night, and the road stretched up the hillside ahead of them, black, lonely, and deathly quiet. Cecily glanced at Baxter's stern face, which was almost hidden by the brim of his homburg.

She was very glad he'd decided to accompany her, though

she had never doubted him for one moment. Poor Baxter. Little had he known what he was taking on when he'd made that last promise to James.

She looked back at her manager's face. He actually looked quite dashing in that hat. So much more fashionable than the bowler he wore in the daytime. She'd never pass a comment, of course, because it would embarrass him dreadfully.

He chose that moment to turn his head, and found her studying him. Disconcerted to have been caught, Cecily covered her momentary confusion by saying, "I am so glad it isn't raining."

He looked at her as if she had said something outrageous. "I imagine the George and Dragon will be closed when we get there," he said stiffly.

"Yes, I do believe it will be."

"And locked up, I would suppose."

"Undoubtedly."

Leaning forward, so as not to let Samuel hear his words, Baxter said quietly, "I do wish you would reconsider, madam. The public house is not a seemly place for a lady to pay a visit. I cannot imagine what people will say when you arrive there."

"The George and Dragon is not just a public house," Cecily muttered. "It's an inn, and respectable people, including women, stay there."

"It is, nevertheless, still a public house. It will seem most improper for you to enter it."

"Piffle! You worry too much. Who is going to see me, pray, now that the establishment is closed down for the night?"

He stared at her for a long moment. "Perhaps you could explain to me how you intend to ask questions without being seen?"

"I am not going to ask questions. I am going to search the body." In spite of her strong tone, she felt a shiver of apprehension as she spoke the words.

Baxter was so shocked he began spluttering. "That's

preposterous! You simply cannot interfere in this manner. It's unthinkable."

"I quite agree," Cecily said with a sigh. "I must admit I have certain qualms about it. Apart from the physical revulsion I shall no doubt feel, there is also the matter of interfering with due process of the law. But I really see no other option. As I said, the inspector is extremely unlikely to take me into his confidence, so what else can I do?"

"You can let the police handle it in the proper manner, as I have begged you to do."

"If I could be sure they would handle it in the proper manner, I would be glad to do so." She shook her head. "We have been over all this before, Baxter. I see no point in repeating it all. Don't worry, I will leave everything as I found it. They will have no idea I have been there. Unless someone sees me, of course."

Baxter managed to look even more forbidding. "Inspector Cranshaw will be most displeased if he finds you there."

"I'm sure he will," Cecily said grimly, "but I do not intend to leave anything to chance. I want to ensure that Madeline is treated fairly, and I can only do that if I know as much as the inspector does."

"I'm quite sure the inspector will obey the letter of the law—"

"Baxter, you know how people feel about Madeline. She is treated with suspicion wherever she goes, by a good many people, simply because she is different. Because of her special talents, the villagers believe she is a witch, while the police believe she is a gypsy. And we all know how the police treat gypsies. I'm afraid that Madeline may be prejudged and will be helpless to defend herself. I know how intimidating Inspector Cranshaw can be."

"May I suggest, madam, that you have never been intimidated by anyone in your life."

Surprised by this personal comment, Cecily smiled. "That's where you are wrong, Baxter. I'm often intimidated by you."

He straightened abruptly, as if shocked by her answer.

Apparently at a loss for words, he turned his head toward the sea, presenting his strong profile.

Yes, Cecily thought, tucking her gloved hands beneath the folds of her cape, she was very glad he'd decided to accompany her.

The lights in the public and saloon bars were doused when Samuel reined in the bay a short distance from the George and Dragon. With a whispered word to the young footman to wait for them, Baxter dismounted from the trap and waited to help Cecily down.

Placing her hand on his arm, she stepped onto the quiet road and glanced a trifle apprehensively at the darkened inn. "Did you say the dead man was in the parlor?" she whispered, standing as close to Baxter as propriety allowed.

"Yes, madam." He looked down at her, his face expressionless beneath the brim of his hat. "I don't suppose you would consider waiting in the trap while I investigate the area first?"

"We have no time for that. We must be quick, before the inspector arrives."

"As I thought." He looked up at Samuel, who sat with his face averted and his back ramrod stiff in the front seat. "Perhaps it would be better if you moved to the shadows of the trees over there," he told the young man. "We shall not be long."

Samuel touched his cap, flicked his whip lightly on the bay's back, and walked it over to the trees at the edge of the field.

"Come on, then," Cecily said, starting off for the inn. She reached the main door with Baxter close behind her. Looking back at him, she whispered, "It's locked."

"Yes, madam."

"Is there another way in without disturbing anybody?"

"I doubt it, madam. Not without breaking the law."

"Baxter, we are most likely breaking the law just by being here investigating the scene of a crime, before the police have arrived. I do believe it might be a little late to worry about it now."

"I am not at all happy about this," Baxter muttered. "Not at all."

"I take note of your objections, Baxter. However, I insist that you try a window or something. If I can sneak in and out again without being seen, we can avoid getting into any trouble."

"There is a possible entrance that might not be locked, but it would be taking a grave risk," Baxter said, glancing back at the trees where the trap now stood hidden from the road.

"Show it to me."

"I would prefer that you wait here while I investigate."

He really could be most stubborn, Cecily thought, beginning to lose patience. "No, Baxter. I will investigate while you keep watch."

"But, madam—"

"We do not have time to argue. If someone should arrive before I can leave, it would be better for you to be standing outside. You can offer some explanation, giving me a chance to escape."

She waited, nerves tingling, while he struggled with indecision, then she let out her breath when he gave a brief nod.

"Very well. Though what kind of explanation I can offer is beyond me."

"You'll think of something," Cecily assured him. She followed him around the corner of the stone building to the back, across the uneven cobblestones to a small door set low in the wall.

"It leads to the coal cellar," Baxter whispered, "but there is also a passageway to the left of the stairs that leads to the main hall. The door on the right is the parlor, where they have laid out the dead man." He lifted the latch quietly, and the door opened with a quiet squeak.

"Well done, Bax," Cecily whispered. "Now keep watch out here. I shall be as quick as possible."

"There is a window in the parlor, overlooking the vegetable plot. If I hear the police arriving, or any signs of you being disturbed, I'll tap on the window three times."

"Yes. That's a good idea."

"You must leave immediately. If you come out this way, you should be undetected. It's doubtful anyone will come around the back of the inn."

"Don't worry, I shall be perfectly fine." She opened the door farther and stepped into the narrow space beyond it.

"It's very dark," Baxter whispered behind her. "You will have to feel your way along. Please, madam, I beg you to be careful. Remember, the stairs are on the right, the passage-way is on the left."

Feeling her way along the wall with her hand, Cecily shuffled first one foot forward, then the next. She should have brought a lamp, she thought a little belatedly. But then she ran the risk of the light being seen.

Her fingers brushed against a doorway on her left, and she slipped through it into a wider passageway with a sharply sloping ceiling. At the end of it a door stood ajar, and light spilled through the opening. At last she could see.

She stood very still, listening intently. Overhead the floor creaked as someone walked across it, and she held her breath. She hoped no one was standing guard over the body, though she couldn't imagine why someone should do so.

Very slowly she edged toward the door and looked out into the hall. It was empty. Opposite her, she saw the securely bolted main door of the inn. The two doors on the left were closed, as was the right, which Baxter had said was the parlor.

Looking up, Cecily realized she had emerged from a door beneath the staircase. Again the floorboards creaked, and she froze, praying that whoever was causing the noise was not coming down the stairs to the hall.

After a moment the creaking subsided, and she relaxed. She quickly crossed the hallway to the parlor door and turned the handle.

To her immense relief, it wasn't locked, and she pushed the door open and stepped inside the parlor. Her eyes went at once to the body lying on the chaise longue. Someone had covered it with a sheet. Even so, her stomach rebelled at the sight.

She had seen a dead body before, but that experience didn't make viewing this one any easier. A small lamp burned on a table nearby, and Cecily gently closed the door behind her before crossing the floor to the chaise.

The dim light cast the corners of the room in darkness, but she could see the body quite clearly. For a moment she faltered. No matter how strong the reason, one did not break the law easily. Not unless one was criminally minded, that is.

Then she thought about Madeline, perhaps hung for a crime she did not commit. Bracing herself, Cecily lifted off the sheet.

Deliberately keeping her gaze from the dead man's face, she searched the pockets. She found a small coin purse and several folded pound notes. In another pocket she found a folded slip of paper. Resisting the urge to look at it right away, she continued her search. She found a comb and an opened packet of pipe tobacco in his jacket pocket.

Digging her fingers into the pocket of his waistcoat, she felt a small piece of card and drew it out. Holding it under the lamp, she read the face of it. A surge of triumph ended in a satisfied sigh.

In her hand she held a train ticket from London to Wellercombe. It bore today's date, and there was only one train from London. The victim had arrived in Badgers End after the police had taken Madeline in for questioning.

With such clear evidence, she felt sure the police would arrive at the same conclusion. She would replace the ticket in the pocket, where the inspector was bound to find it.

Feeling a great deal easier in her mind, Cecily quickly replaced the items she'd removed from the dead man's pockets. She was about to replace the slip of paper, then decided to take a quick peek.

She leaned forward with the paper in her hand so that the light from the lamp fell across it. She could make out three names scribbled on it. *Colin Bickley. Billy Donaldson.* She felt a little thrill of excitement as she stared at the names. This was far better than anything she'd expected. This could lead her to the solution of the puzzle, making sure that Madeline's name would be cleared.

Then her gaze moved down to the third name. For a moment she stared at it. Then she spoke the name aloud in a shocked whisper. "Ian Rossiter."

Her mind whirled with confused thoughts. She glanced at the dead man's face, then looked back at the slip of paper with a shudder. The list made no sense.

A sharp tap on the window brought her head up sharply. She heard a second tap and then the third. With a hiss of breath she stooped to pick up the sheet and threw it over the cold, still body. Then she hurried to the door and slipped through it.

Outside she could hear the clatter of hooves and a hoarse shout of command. Her heart lurched anxiously as she thought about Baxter out there. Had someone seen him? Was the inspector already demanding to know why he was there?

Swiftly she sped across the carpet to the door under the staircase. As she tugged it open, she heard heavy footsteps pounding on the stairs above her. Dragging her skirt through the narrow doorway with both hands, Cecily slipped through and closed the door.

She was in thick, black darkness, and for a moment felt disoriented. The parlor door had been on the right, and the passageway on the left. That meant the passageway was now on her right . . . no, the stairs to the cellar were on her right . . . that meant they would be on her left going back . . .

The thunder of footsteps overhead signaled more people on the stairs. Cecily shuffled forward, going a good deal faster on her way out than she had on her way in. She found the doorway to the coal cellars and prayed she wouldn't trip down the stairs.

Then she felt the cold, swift rush of night air. "Baxter," she whispered urgently, "are you there?"

"Thank God. Hurry, madam. If we leave now we can possibly get away without being seen."

She stumbled as she rushed out of the door and felt Baxter's firm grip on her arm. He motioned for her to be quiet with a finger at his lips, then led the way around the building to the front.

Cecily had a very bad moment when he paused suddenly and drew back, but then he bent his head and said softly, "It appears that everyone is indoors. I think it is safe to run for the trap."

Lifting her skirt clear of the ground, Cecily whispered back, "I'm ready."

He lifted his head as if in silent prayer, then strode out into the silent street, keeping to the shadows at the side of the road. Staying close behind him, Cecily trotted to keep up. She was quite out of breath when she heard the soft whinny of the bay standing under the trees.

Baxter, abandoning proprieties for once, bundled her unceremoniously into the trap and leapt in beside her. "Try not to make too much noise," he told Samuel, who merely nodded as if the escapade was an everyday occurrence, and walked the bay back onto the road.

Cecily had never noticed before how loudly the trap creaked. Promising herself she would have it oiled as soon as possible, she straightened her clothes and sat back in the seat. She didn't relax, however, until they were once more jogging along the Esplanade back to the hotel.

"Thank you, Baxter," she said as they passed under the orange lamps once more. "I appreciate your help tonight. I shan't forget it."

"Neither shall I," Baxter murmured with feeling. "I do hope the effort proved successful."

"Yes, most certainly so. I found a train ticket in the pocket that proves the victim arrived in Wellercombe after Madeline was taken in by the police. In which case, she couldn't be responsible for his death."

Baxter nodded slowly. "I would agree. However, though I dislike throwing cold water on your theory, that in itself does not prove Madeline innocent of the first two deaths."

"I thought of that also. But it will almost certainly weaken the case against her. It is reasonable to assume that whoever killed the third man also killed the other two. All we have to do is find the reason."

"That may prove difficult."

"I think I found something that might help. Something that I'm afraid is very alarming. A slip of paper with the names of Colin Bickley and Billy Donaldson scribbled on it."

"Ah, well that should prove there is a connection somewhere. But why is that alarming?"

Cecily frowned. "There was another name on there. Ian Rossiter. I'm very much afraid, Baxter, that Ian might also be marked for death."

CHAPTER

❖14❖

Cecily heard Baxter draw in a sharp breath. "Then we must warn Ian of the danger."

"I agree." She shook her head. "I just can't make sense of this. The fact that the stranger carried the names of the two dead men would indicate that he was the murderer. Yet if so, why would he be killed himself, apparently by the same method? And why is Ian on the list?"

"Perhaps he can enlighten us. Did you get the man's name?"

"No, I didn't have time to do a thorough search."

"I imagine there has to be a connection between them of some kind."

"I would agree. I'll have to question Ian when we get back to the hotel."

Baxter cleared his throat. Now that the immediate danger was over, he had reverted back to his shield of etiquette. "If

I might suggest, madam, it would be infinitely preferable if you were to allow the police to question Ian, as they will surely do once they begin their investigation. Once they see the list for themselves, I'm sure they will be able to work things out to a satisfactory conclusion."

"I would tend to agree with you again, Baxter," Cecily said demurely, "if it were not for one thing." She held up the slip of paper and waved it under his nose. "They don't have the list. I do."

"For heaven's sake, madam!" Baxter's words came out in an explosion of wrath. His efforts to refrain from giving full rein to it were clearly visible on his face.

Cecily glanced up at Samuel's stiff back and laid a finger to her lips. "We'll continue this conversation in the library," she said softly. Raising her voice, she added, "It is decidedly chilly out here, Baxter. I shall be glad to return to the warmth of the hotel."

They passed under a lamp, and Baxter tilted his head, allowing his icy gaze to slice through her. She had expected this reaction from him, and it was probably justified. Even so, she squirmed under his reproach.

She didn't like upsetting him this way. She knew very well how frustrating it must be for him. He was charged with taking care of her, yet because of his position was helpless to control her actions. For a man of Baxter's sense of loyalty and duty, he was in an intolerable situation.

Most of his discomfort was his own doing, Cecily reminded herself, in an attempt to assuage her guilt. She was perfectly willing to relax the rules. He was the one who refused to unbend.

She felt more than a little thankful when the trap pulled up in front of the main steps to the Pennyfoot. She hoped that Baxter's temper had cooled a little. She hated to see his fierce struggles to contain it. Anger was like laughter; it was better let free.

Holding her skirt above her ankles, she preceded him up the steps, feeling the heat of his disapproval on her back all the way up. Reaching the top landing, she paused, waiting for him to open the door.

"You know what we need, Baxter?" she said brightly, watching him take the heavy key from its hiding place behind a loose brick. "We need a doorman. I think that would add a distinct flair to the place, don't you? I think we should be able to afford one, for the next Season at least. I shall have to see about hiring one."

"Yes, madam." Baxter unlocked the massive door, pushed it open, and stepped back.

She didn't look at his face as she stepped into the welcome warmth of the lobby. She waited while he returned the key to its secret home and then shot the bolts on the door.

"I do hope Mrs. Parmentier has returned for the night," she said, glancing at the grandfather clock in the corner of the lobby. "I can't imagine where she goes all by herself after dark."

"Perhaps she has a secret rendezvous with someone."

Cecily's eyes opened wide. "Baxter! How very unlike you to suggest such a thing. The poor woman recently lost her husband—it would be most disrespectful for her to take a lover so quickly."

Amused, she noticed Baxter's flushed cheeks, which she was quite sure had nothing to do with the chill of the night.

"Please accept my apology, madam. I can only attribute my thoughtlessness to a most disturbing evening."

Cecily turned away before he could see her grimace. Trust him to neatly turn the tables on her again. "Well, shall it be the kitchen for a hot cup of tea and perhaps a splash of brandy to calm your nerves, or would you prefer the library?"

"The tea sounds very appealing, madam, though the brandy won't be necessary."

"Maybe not for you," Cecily said as she led the way to the stairs, "but I would certainly enjoy it."

For once, he made no comment as he followed her down the stairs.

*   *   *

Mrs. Chubb had been terrified of what she might find when she'd rushed into Gertie's room earlier that night. She could only pray that the girl hadn't already swallowed the mixture.

The light from the hallway spilled over the polished floorboards and across the narrow cot in the corner of the room. Mrs. Chubb's first thought when she saw Gertie's inert form lying on her back, mouth open and eyes shut, was that she was too late.

She let out a dreadful moan and clamped a hand over her mouth. With a shaking hand, she dragged the matches from the pocket of her apron and lit the candle, which stood on the small round table at the bedside.

Now she could see the housemaid's face more clearly. It didn't look blue. It looked a little pale, but it didn't look blue. Picking up the candle, Mrs. Chubb leaned closer, in an effort to see if there was any movement of breathing beneath the sheet tucked under Gertie's chin.

Closer and closer she leaned, and then Gertie let out a loud, rattling snore.

Startled, Mrs. Chubb's arm jerked, tipping some of the melted wax onto the sleeping girl's shoulder. Luckily the sheet prevented it from burning her skin, but it was hot enough to wake her up with an earsplitting shriek.

Thoroughly unnerved, Mrs. Chubb jumped backward, smashing into the little table, which rocked back and forth on its three spindly legs, then toppled to the floor with a loud crash.

Gertie screamed and shot up in the bed as footsteps pounded along the hallway.

Ian's face appeared in the doorway. "What the hell is going on in here?"

Recovering with astonishing speed, Mrs. Chubb shot across the room and shoved him down the hallway. "Whatever next," she said breathlessly. "You should know better than to enter a lady's boudoir when she's undressed and in her bed."

Belatedly remembering Gertie's condition, she reflected

that it probably wasn't the first time. Still, as long as she was around to preserve the proprieties, she wasn't about to allow any hanky-panky in her domain.

Ian looked taken aback, but thankfully didn't confirm her suspicions. "What did she scream for, then? Is she all right? I thought she was being flipping murdered in her bed."

Mrs. Chubb shook her head. "Just a nightmare, I expect." She could hear Gertie moaning in fright in her bedroom and was anxious to get back and comfort her. "You go back to the kitchen and wait there," she told Ian. "You've had a terrible night. There's a bottle of Michel's best brandy in the cupboard. He won't miss a tablespoon or so, I daresay. As soon as I've settled Gertie down, I'll come and let you know."

Ian looked most surprised at this generous offer, though doubt lingered on his face as he nodded. "Right ho, Mrs. Chubb, thanks. I'll do that."

She didn't wait to see him leave, but hurried back to the bedroom to console Gertie, who was rocking back and forth in bed, clutching the blankets in front of her.

"I'm sorry, love," Mrs. Chubb said, patting one of the shaking shoulders. "I didn't mean to scare you, but I thought . . ." Her voice trailed off. She'd forgotten that Gertie didn't know about the third death or Madeline's detention.

"Scared the blooming daylights out of me, you did," Gertie said, her face accusing in the flickering candlelight. "Whatcha go and do that for?" Before Mrs. Chubb could answer, she added, "And what's Ian doing here? I thought he'd gone down to the pub for the night."

Deciding that the girl would hear all about it in the morning, Mrs. Chubb related the latest events.

"Strewth," Gertie said when she was finished. "Did you really think Madeline had poisoned me?"

"Well, not intentionally, of course," Mrs. Chubb admitted, feeling very uncomfortable. "And now that I have time to think about it, I can see how ridiculous it is, but when Ian blurted all that out about the police taking Madeline in for questioning, the shock of it all addled my brain. I was so shook up over what Ian was telling me I wasn't thinking straight."

"Well, I think there are some people around here who are a lot more suspicious than Madeline," Gertie said, sliding back down onto her pillow.

Mrs. Chubb's ears pricked up. "Like who?"

"Well, like that Black Widow for one."

The housekeeper tutted. "You still going on about that poor woman? All she wants is to be left alone to mourn her dead husband, that's all. There's nothing strange about that."

"Well, I think there's a lot strange about that. Always going out at night and coming back late. And hiding behind that thick black veil." Gertie shuddered. "Gives me the creeps, she does. It's like talking to someone with no face. I hate talking to someone when I can't see their eyes. You never know where they're looking, do you?"

"All widows wear veils when they're in mourning," Mrs. Chubb said firmly. "I did."

"Not that thick, I bet you didn't. I know madam didn't. You could still see a bit of her face, at any rate."

"Well, I'm sure once she takes off her widows weeds she'll seem perfectly ordinary." Mrs. Chubb leaned over and blew out the candle. "Now go to sleep, and stop worrying about poor Mrs. Parmentier. You'll be having nightmares."

"I've already had one tonight," Gertie muttered.

Mrs. Chubb reached the door and started to close it.

"You know something that's really strange?" Gertie said from her dark corner of the room.

"What's that?"

"If she's supposed to be mourning so bad, why isn't she still wearing a wedding ring?"

Mrs. Chubb frowned. "I never noticed."

"Well, I did. When she took the tray from me. I noticed her hands. Big they were, and she weren't wearing no rings." Gertie yawned. "She didn't even have a mark of one. I remember when me mum took hers off, she had a dent in her finger where the ring had been. For months."

Mrs. Chubb had no answer for that one. "Go to sleep," she said instead. "Good night, Gertie."

Gertie mumbled an answering, "G'night," and the housekeeper gently closed the door.

She tried not to think about Gertie's remarks as she hurried back to the kitchen. There were enough horrible things going on without worrying about something as silly as a wedding ring.

She pushed open the door of the kitchen and peeked inside. Ian was sitting at the table, his head on his arms, sound asleep. Shaking her head, Mrs. Chubb backed out again and let the door swing to. He might as well sleep there by the warm stove for a while. No doubt he'd find his way home once he woke up.

She passed Gertie's door again on the way to her own room. The possibility that Ian might spend the rest of the night in Gertie's bed occurred to her, and she almost went back to turf him out.

Then she shrugged. What the eye didn't see, the heart didn't grieve over. Besides, by all accounts the damage was already done. Muttering to herself about the scandalous behavior of today's youth, Mrs. Chubb retired to her room.

Cecily saw Ian asleep at the table and paused in the doorway of the kitchen. Baxter, coming up behind her, bumped into her and began apologizing profusely. Ian lifted his head and blinked sleepily at Cecily.

"Oh, sorry, Mrs. Sinclair. Must have dozed off for a while."

Cecily's eyes strayed to the brandy bottle standing on the table and said dryly, "I wonder why?"

Ian sprang to his feet, gathering up his cap in his hands. "Mrs. Chubb said it was all right to have a drop. That's all I had, a drop in me tea. Honest."

Cecily ignored Baxter's impatient huff of breath. "That's all right, Ian. As a matter of fact, I'm pleased to find you here. There's something important I wish to discuss with you."

"I'll put the kettle on, madam," Baxter offered, moving across to the stove.

Cecily sent him a smile of thanks, then sat down with a sigh of relief on one of the chairs. "I asked you the other day," she said to Ian, who remained standing, "if Mr. Donaldson and Mr. Bickley had anything in common, other than that they worked together."

"Yes, mum. I told you I didn't think so."

Cecily leaned forward, peering up into Ian's anxious face. "I have something else to ask you, Ian, and it is very important that you tell me the truth. I want to know if you had any dealings with the two dead men. Anything at all."

Ian shook his head. "No, mum, I didn't. Bickley was my boss, of course, and Donaldson worked on my shift, but other than that, I had no truck with them. They was sort of on the opposite side to me, weren't they. I mean, I'm one of the villagers, and they was the strangers, like. They weren't one of us."

Cecily sighed. She had no doubt that Ian was telling the truth. "I just don't know what to make of all this."

"Well, there's something else, mum. Something I haven't told the police as yet."

Cecily looked up sharply, while Baxter paused in the act of filling the kettle.

"I seen him before," Ian said, looking unhappy. "The third man's name is Ted Sparks. He's a reporter from one of them London newspapers. He was down here a couple of weeks ago, asking a lot of questions. Said he was doing a story on the lighthouse project."

Disturbed by this news, Cecily exchanged a worried glance with Baxter. "Why didn't you tell the police that?" she asked Ian.

He looked even more upset. "I don't know. I suppose I was worried, like. The bloke was asking for me, in the pub. He asked Gerry if I was there. I didn't like the nosy bugger, so I went into the saloon till he left."

"Do you have any idea what he wanted to speak with you about?"

Ian shook his head. "I heard him say he'd asked Dolly Matthews where to find me, and she'd sent him to the George. I don't know what he wanted. When he was down before he was asking me a lot of questions that I didn't think were any of his business."

"What kind of questions?"

"About me private life. What I did in me spare time. Nothing to do with the job. I told him to get lost."

"And do you remember if he talked to Mr. Bickley and Mr. Donaldson at that time?"

He shrugged. "He talked to a lot of blokes. I didn't take that much notice." He looked at Cecily with appeal in his eyes. "I couldn't tell the police. They might think I done him in. I don't have too good a record in the city, but I tell you this, mum, I never killed no one. Never. And if I had, I wouldn't bloody poison them. There's a lot quicker ways than that."

Baxter tutted as he measured tea into the teapot, but Cecily ignored him. "Ian," she said, "in view of what you've told me, I think it would be most advisable if you stay here at the hotel until the police have this matter cleared up. Since it appears you are connected with the murdered men, you could be in some danger."

A swift look of alarm crossed his face. "I don't know how I'm connected, mum, I really don't. I never seen Sparks before he came down to the project. I swear I didn't."

"Nevertheless, it would seem you are involved somehow. Until we can find exactly where everything fits, I would feel better if you were here under my roof. You can have your old room back, since it's empty. Now that you are working for me again, it will make things easier for you."

Ian looked unconvinced. "You won't tell the police, will you? I don't want no trouble with the law."

Cecily regarded him with a worried frown. "I may not have to. I am quite sure that Gerry will have informed the inspector that Mr. Sparks was asking for you. We shall just have to wait and see what transpires in the morning. In the meantime, I suggest you try to get some sleep."

"Thank you, mum." His expression suggested it would be a wasted effort. "If it's all right with you, I'll stay the night and collect my things from the boardinghouse in the morning."

"I think that would be a very good idea, Ian."

Murmuring a subdued "Good night," Ian left the kitchen.

As the door swung to behind him, Baxter said quietly, "I am thankful you saw fit not to mention finding the list."

"I didn't think it was necessary," Cecily said, feeling suddenly very tired herself. "It would only complicate matters if he knew about our little excursion tonight. As long as he is here at the hotel, he should be safe. I should think after everything he's been through he'll be most careful about what he eats and drinks."

Baxter nodded. "As will we all. I imagine this will be very bad for business at the George and Dragon."

"I'm afraid," Cecily said slowly, "that if we don't find out who is behind all this, it will be very bad for Badgers End and the Pennyfoot Hotel. Between us and the police, Baxter, I hope we can stop this fiend before he murders someone else."

CHAPTER

❉15❉

"So what do you intend to do about the list?" Baxter asked. He had his back to her, bending over the stove while he stoked the coals.

Cecily made a face at him, which he couldn't see. She knew he wouldn't let the matter rest. "I shall have to work things out for myself, I suppose."

Baxter straightened and turned to look at her, his expression stiff with disapproval. "I feel very strongly that you should hand it over to the police. What you have done amounts to tampering with the evidence, and I fear that could have grave consequences for you."

"Which is why I cannot let the police know I have it," Cecily said calmly.

"I can't imagine what possessed you to take it in the first place."

"With all the excitement of the police arriving, and in my

anxiety to escape without being seen, I didn't have time to put it back."

"Perhaps we could say that Ian came across it when he discovered the body," Baxter said, looking a little desperate.

"I think Ian is in quite enough trouble without us making things worse for him." Cecily took out the folded slip of paper from her pocket and looked at it again.

"I'm afraid there's nothing for it, Baxter, but to work this out ourselves. Inspector Cranshaw has made it quite clear that he will not tolerate me becoming involved in police business again. As you well know, I can't afford to cross swords with the police. So far they have turned a blind eye to some of our more . . . nefarious activities in the hotel."

"That is because of our exclusive clientele. They would not wish to offend the upper crust without good cause."

"Precisely. No one is more aware than I, however, that we are treading an extremely thin line. What with the gambling belowstairs and the flagrant promiscuity that abounds in the boudoirs, I'm afraid the Pennyfoot would suffer greatly from the resulting publicity. If we step too far over that line, the inspector will be able to find numerous reasons to shut the Pennyfoot down."

"I am also painfully aware of that fact, madam."

Steam boiled from the kettle, and Baxter poured the bubbling water onto the tea leaves.

Cecily watched him as he took down cups and saucers from the cupboard. It wasn't often she allowed him to wait on her like this. It felt very . . . cozy.

"You also know, Baxter," she said, "that the people around here do not trust the police. They do, however, trust me. The villagers of Badgers End will talk to me and tell me things they wouldn't dream of confiding to the police. If the answers lie somewhere in the village, as I think they must do, I have a much better chance of finding them than Inspector Cranshaw or P. C. Northcott."

"Especially that simpleton," Baxter muttered. "Very well, I see no alternative at the moment. But I feel most emphatically that had you not kept the list, we would not be in this predicament now."

"I told you, Bax, I simply didn't have time to put it back."

Baxter's harumph signified his disbelief of that statement.

Deciding it was time to change the subject, Cecily yawned. "Well, it is a long way past my bedtime, and I am ready to fall asleep at the drop of a hat. So if you would please pour me a cup of tea, I can then be off to my bed."

As Baxter set the fragrant, steaming cup down in front of her, Cecily had a sudden thought. "I knew there was something else I wanted to do. Colonel Fortescue. Ian's arrival with the news of the latest victim put the entire thing out of my head." She looked up to find Baxter's quizzical gaze upon her. "I will try to find him first thing in the morning. I just have a feeling that for once he might be able to tell me something useful."

She ignored Baxter's puzzled frown and sipped her tea. This was one time she intended to keep her thoughts to herself. At least until she'd had time to talk to the colonel. The chances were that his nonsensical stories would be of no help to her at all. On the other hand, he might just be the person to put her one step closer to the solution.

As it turned out, something else happened the next morning to delay Cecily's chat with the colonel. From her bedroom window she spotted the police carriage outside the front steps of the hotel. By the time she had hurried down the stairs and reached the lobby, the carriage had left.

Bidding a bright good morning to one of her guests as she crossed the lobby, Cecily wondered what the police had wanted and why no one had informed her of their presence. She had an uneasy feeling that it could have something to do with Ian.

She hurried down the stairs to the kitchen, and before she reached the door she could hear Gertie's wailing. Pushing the door open, she saw the housemaid seated on a chair, wiping her eyes on her apron.

Mrs. Chubb hovered over her, while Michel stood at the stove, crashing saucepans around to show his irritation. The chef's black mustache twitched, and his dark eyes flashed as he brandished a wooden spoon. His tall chef's hat bobbed back and forth while he muttered to himself

He swept off the hat when Cecily entered the kitchen, then after she'd acknowledged his greeting, he pulled it back on again and went back to his noisy administrations at the stove.

Gertie dragged herself off the chair and stood there sniveling.

"What happened?" Cecily asked a worried-looking Mrs. Chubb.

Before she could answer, Gertie let out a loud wail. "It's Ian, mum, they've taken him to the clink." The last word was almost drowned by her loud sobs.

"Pull yourself together, girl," Mrs. Chubb said briskly. "He hasn't gone to prison, he's just gone to answer some questions, like Madeline."

Gertie shook her head, her sobs getting louder.

Mrs. Chubb looked exasperated, and Cecily touched her arm. "Let me try," she said as a saucepan crashed loudly behind her.

Gertie's sobs subsided a little when Cecily said in a kind voice, "Now, Gertie, please tell me what happened."

It took the housemaid several seconds to control herself enough to answer, and when she did, her words were punctuated by sobs. "A blooming bobby came and got him. Said the inspector wanted to talk to him about finding the body."

Cecily patted the tearful Gertie on the arm. "Now, I'm quite sure there is nothing to worry about. Ian will simply answer the inspector's questions, and he will be back before you know it."

"But . . . but . . . the bobby said they was going to ask Ian about all that damage what was done up at the project . . ." Whatever she said next was lost in another storm of weeping.

Mrs. Chubb shook her head. "I don't know whatever's

got into the girl. She never carries on like this as a rule, not our Gertie."

"Is there something else worrying you?" Cecily asked, wondering if perhaps the housemaid knew more than she was telling.

Gertie's mouth opened and closed, then she blurted out, "I'm scared . . . they're going to find out . . . about the smuggling."

A shocked silence followed her words as Cecily stared at the stricken girl. Then, in the background, Michel muttered a soft, *"Sacré bleu."*

Gertie slapped a hand over her mouth, her horrified eyes staring back at Cecily. "Oh, dear Gawd," she mumbled, "what have I gone and done?"

"Smuggling?" Mrs. Chubb's voice rose several notches. "Smuggling? What are you talking about, girl?"

Gertie looked from one to another, as if seeking escape from whatever was coming next.

"I think you'd better explain," Cecily said quietly. "Sit down, Gertie, and tell us what this is all about."

Gertie plopped back on the chair, her face as white as a bag of flour. "I swore I wouldn't tell . . . but that was before they took Ian off, and if they find out about it, Ian said they'd put him in the clink, and I won't see him . . ."

She began to sob again, and Mrs. Chubb clicked her tongue.

"Perhaps a nice hot cup of tea, Mrs. Chubb?" Cecily suggested.

The housekeeper looked disapproving, but went to fill the kettle.

"Now," Cecily said, "who has been smuggling what?"

"Dick Scroggins, that's who. Ian says he's been smuggling brandy in from France. That's why he don't want the lighthouse built. Ian says it's him what done the mess up at the project."

"I see." Cecily frowned. "And Ian has been helping him?"

Mrs. Chubb snorted in disgust. "Silly young man. I thought he had more sense than that."

Michel, who had become very quiet, murmured agreement.

"Only with the smuggling, mum, I swear," Gertie said earnestly. "Ian never had nothing to do with the damage done on the lighthouse. Put him out of a job, it did. He was mad about it."

"Well, let's hope the police believe that," Cecily said, not sure what to believe herself. "But it's not going to help Ian by getting all upset. We will have to wait and see what happens. Then we'll know what to do."

Finally smothering her sobs, Gertie said between hiccups, "I'm so worried about him, mum, that's all. You never know with the bloody police, what they'll do next."

"Well, I don't think Ian has much to worry about if he didn't have anything to do with the sabotage at the lighthouse," Cecily said firmly. "I'm quite sure he isn't responsible for the deaths of those men, which is what the police are concerned about right now. As soon as he's answered the inspector's questions, rest assured they'll send him back here."

"I hope so, mum," Gertie said in a small voice.

"Well, now, I think it's time you took a tray up to Mrs. Parmentier," Mrs. Chubb said, looking as if she'd like to strangle Gertie. "Michel has it all ready for you."

"I have it ready a long time," Michel said in his thick French accent. "It will not be so 'ot, but is not my fault."

"Don't worry, Michel," Cecily said with a smile, "I'm sure Mrs. Parmentier will not complain."

"Gawd, I bloody hope not," Gertie muttered, getting to her feet. "I can't take much more of this, I can tell you."

Mrs. Chubb raised her eyebrows and shook her head.

"Send me word as soon as Ian returns," Cecily told the housekeeper. "I'd like to talk to him."

"Yes, mum, I'll send Gertie up right away."

Cecily threw a last glance at the subdued housemaid and left the kitchen.

At least Ian should be safe with the police, Cecily thought as she climbed the stairs to the lobby. Maybe she should have warned him about the list last night. She had thought at the time that the fewer people who knew about it the better, but now she wasn't so sure she had done the right thing.

She could only hope that Ian would come straight back to the hotel, in which case she would tell him as soon as he arrived. Feeling a little better, she headed across the lobby for the hallway. She wanted to speak to Colonel Fortescue, and she knew where to find him.

The colonel sat on a comfortable chair in the lounge, buried behind a newspaper from which a cloud of aromatic smoke rose in the air.

Cecily paused in the doorway and sniffed appreciatively. She hadn't enjoyed a cigar in a while, and she was almost tempted to ask the colonel for one of his. Judging from the smell, he smoked a very good brand. Probably Cuban. Suppressing the urge, she tapped on the door to let him know she was there.

"Excuse me, Colonel," she said loudly, "I wonder if I might have a word with you?"

The newspaper rattled as the colonel lowered it and peered over it in surprise. "Well, of course, old bean." He got clumsily to his feet. "What can I do for you?"

Thankful to find him alone, Cecily entered the room, leaving the door ajar.

"Wanted to have a chat with you in any case," the colonel said before she could speak. "Almost Guy Fawkes, you know. Just thought I might be able to help out, what? What?"

She'd forgotten all about it, Cecily thought with a stab of guilt. With all this excitement, it had gone clear out of her head.

"I haven't had time to finalize the arrangements yet, Colonel, but I thank you for your offer. It's most kind of you."

"You are going to do the fireworks, old girl, aren't you?"

The colonel wagged his finger. "They're all expecting it, you know. Every year we've had fireworks for Guy Fawkes. Can't let them down, old bean."

He cleared his throat several times. "I understand. With Sinclair gone, must be a damn rough ride for you, so I'll be happy to set the blighters up for you. Can't set them off, though, I'm afraid. Not very good around explosives anymore. Got a bit of a dickey heart, you know."

Cecily smiled in sympathy. "Please don't worry, Colonel. I'm quite sure Baxter can take care of it."

Blinking furiously, the colonel nodded. "Oh, jolly good, yes, what? It will be smashing fun, watching it all from the courtyard with everyone. Champagne flowing and all that rot, what?"

Which is what he was really interested in, Cecily thought wryly. "Yes, of course. I'm sure we'll all have a good time. Now, I wanted to ask you about something you mentioned the other day. I believe you saw a man die in the tropics. You said his skin was blue, if I remember?"

"Yes, yes." The colonel crushed his cigar into an ashtray. "Dashed odd, that was. Poor chap must have been in agony. Looked absolutely awful, writhing about on the ground, moaning and—"

"Yes, I am sure," Cecily interrupted hastily. "So you said. I was just wondering, did you by any chance learn the cause of his death?"

Colonel Fortescue's eyebrows went up and down, and he blinked furiously at her. "Not thinking about those chappies who died here in the village, are you? Can't be the same thing, that. Can't be that at all."

"Why do you say that, Colonel?"

The colonel shook his head. "Nasty business, that was. True, poor chap died of poisoning. But it was one of those primitive bastards who live in the jungle. Tiny little nippers, they are. Look as if a breath of wind would blow them away."

Cecily frowned. "I'm sorry, I—"

"Natives, old bean. Ugly as a baboon, but dashed quick

on their feet. Use poisoned darts. Can kill an elephant with one of those pesky things. Just get a stick of bamboo, dip a sliver into the poison, drop it in the end, and . . ." He put an imaginary pipe in his mouth and puffed through his fingers. "Tally ho, down it goes. Deader than a doornail, old girl. Bloody marvelous, that." He coughed. "Oh, beg your pardon."

Cecily barely heard him. She was thinking about something Dr. McDuff had told her. "Tell me, Colonel," she said, "I don't suppose you happen to know the name of the poison they use?"

Colonel Fortescue shook his head. "Haven't a clue, old girl. Some kind of exotic substance, shouldn't wonder."

Cecily nodded. "Well, thank you. I shan't keep you any longer."

She turned to leave, and the colonel said worriedly, "Don't think they followed me here, by any chance?"

Confused, Cecily looked at him. "Who might that be, Colonel?"

"The little savages with the pipes. Should hate to have to go around the hotel ducking at every sound."

Cecily smiled. "I rather doubt it. I'm sure I would have noticed any primitive native warriors running around."

The colonel wagged a finger at her. "You never know, old bean. Never know. Clever little buggers, they are. Just be prepared to duck if you come across one."

"I'll remember that," Cecily promised solemnly, and left him muttering to himself.

Heading for the library, she turned over in her mind everything she'd heard. There was only a slim chance that the men could have been struck by poison darts, of course, but it was a possibility certainly worth investigating. She shut herself in the library and then searched the shelves.

James had acquired several books on the tropics, having spent much of his youth there in the military. Cecily took down three of the heavy books and carried them to the long table. Then she sat herself down and began to go through the pages.

Almost an hour later she finally found what she was looking for. In an article on wild game hunting, she found a reference to the poisoned darts used by the South American Indians. The poison they used was curare, extracted from a tropical vine.

Reading rapidly down the page, she discovered that the poison was harmless and had no effect when swallowed. When injected into the skin, however, a small dose would slow down the heartbeat and put the victim into a deep sleep.

An overdose would be instantly fatal, producing a paralyzing effect. The poison would attack the muscles of the toes, ears, and eyes, then those of the neck and limbs, and finally those involved in respiration. In fatal doses, death was caused by respiratory paralysis.

The last paragraph caused her to catch her breath. Similar to the symptoms of cyanide, it discolored the skin, turning it blue after death.

Gertie tapped on the door of Mrs. Parmentier's room, dreading the moment when the widow would open the door and confront her with that faceless head.

She shifted the heavy tray and got ready to thrust it into the big ugly hands of the woman, so that she could make her escape as soon as possible. She waited and waited, the edges of the tray digging into her palms, but the door remained closed.

Gertie frowned. Was it possible the widow was still asleep? Wouldn't be surprised, all that walking the streets late at night. She'd give anything to know what the woman was up to.

Lifting her knee, she balanced the tray awkwardly with one hand and knocked again, louder this time. Still no answer.

Gertie looked up and down the hallway. Now what? She'd have to take the loaded tray all the way back to the kitchen. Michel would give her hell, as if it was her fault.

She looked down at the grapefruit wedges sprinkled with

sugar, the buttered toast, the soft-boiled egg tucked into its woolen egg cozy, the silver tea service, and her mouth watered. Who would know if she ate it all and took the empty tray back to the kitchen?

The Black Widow would know, that's who. Probably put a blooming spell on her, turn her into a frog. At least she wouldn't be bloody pregnant—

The door opened suddenly, startling Gertie so that she almost dropped the tray. The veiled head appeared in the narrow space, then two large hands crept out to take the tray.

"You've been crying," the husky voice said.

Unnerved, Gertie nodded.

"I take it you're still . . . not feeling well?"

Again Gertie nodded.

"Perhaps I can help. Would you care to come in and talk to me about it?"

Gertie began backing away. "No, ma'am, I don't think . . . I haven't got time . . . I have to be back . . ." Her nerve suddenly deserting her, she turned and fled for the stairs. She didn't stop running until she was safely back in the kitchen, too puffed to tell Mrs. Chubb what had scared her.

CHAPTER

✣ 16 ✣

It was Baxter's half day off, and he had left the hotel for his customary jaunt up to Deep Willow Pond, where he fed the ducks and strolled among the trees to unwind from the constant paperwork and the solving of departmental problems that sometimes seemed endless.

Cecily decided not to wait for his return to discuss her discovery. She was much too anxious to talk to Dr. McDuff. So she ordered the trap and went into the village by herself.

This time she made no pretense of being under the weather, but came straight to the point when the doctor showed her into his surgery. "Dr. McDuff," she said, settling herself on a chair, "I imagine that by now you have examined the third victim. I assume he died from the same poison as the other two?"

"Now, you know I can't discuss this with you—" the doctor began, but Cecily interrupted.

"I need to know this, Dr. McDuff. I do believe I might be able to shed some light on the puzzle."

The doctor stared at her. "Mebbe you should be talking to the inspector, if that's the case."

"I can't talk to the inspector. I think you know why."

Dr. McDuff sighed. "Very well, what do you want to know?"

"Just tell me, if you will, if the third victim died from the same poison."

"Aye, he did."

Satisfied, Cecily nodded. "Then let me tell you about what I learned this morning." She related every word that she could remember of the article, while the doctor listened intently.

When she was finished, Dr. McDuff looked at her, his fierce eyebrows drawn together in a frown. "That's all very interesting, lassie, but I don't see what there is to get excited about. Our victims couldn't have died from curare, it's a tropical plant from South America. What would it be doing here?"

"I can't answer that, Doctor," Cecily admitted, "but it would explain a certain part of the puzzle. The biggest question in all this is how the three men were poisoned. Since these three were the only people affected, it is safe to assume that someone singled them out and administered the poison. But how? If death was instant, as the symptoms suggest, how does that explain the length of time it took Mr. Bickley to die?"

"He could have ingested the poison in his house that night."

"Possible, but unlikely. He was carrying nothing when he left the George and Dragon, so I'm told, and there was no sign of anyone having broken in to tamper with his food."

The doctor's eyes narrowed. "How do you know all this?"

Cecily smiled. "I ask a lot of questions, Doctor. It's amazing what people will tell you when they are excited or intrigued by something."

"Yes, well, I still don't see what all this has to do with a tropical plant."

"You said there were only two possible poisonous plants. I have given you a third."

Dr. McDuff shook his head. "Not a chance. In the first place, the vine doesn't grow in this part of the world. In the second, it is harmless when swallowed. Even if the victims' food or drink had been heavily laced with the stuff, it wouldn't have hurt them."

"But what if it had been injected?" Cecily said quietly.

The doctor studied her with his clear blue eyes. "What are you saying, lassie?"

"I'm saying that three men died after leaving the George and Dragon pub. A pub where there has been a good deal of disagreement going on, including several incidents of fighting among the customers of late."

"That is so, I agree. But I don't understand why you should think a drug could be injected into three men without anyone seeing."

Cecily smiled. "If you remember, Doctor, I told you the natives killed their game, and their enemies, by blowing a poisoned dart through a bamboo pipe."

Still looking puzzled, the doctor nodded.

"Might I also remind you," Cecily said quietly, "that for the past several days, practice has been going on at the pub . . . for a darts match."

She sat back, enjoying the incredulous look spreading over the doctor's face.

After a long pause, Dr. McDuff said slowly, "It's something to think about, I grant you. A slim clue, but nevertheless I should look into it. The first two bodies have been sent to London already, but I can certainly examine this one again to see if I can find a puncture anywhere in the skin."

"Good," Cecily said, rising to her feet. "I agree, it's not a likely solution. Had it not been for the darts match, I would not have considered it. But the one thing that has intrigued me from the beginning of all this is that Mr. Bickley was found outside his cottage without his coat which he had worn that evening. If death had been instantaneous after he'd ingested the poison inside his cottage, how did he get outside?"

"Aye." The doctor stroked his beard. "So you're suggesting someone called him outside and then stuck him with a dart? Though who would have access to such a poison in these parts I can't imagine."

"I'm simply weighing all the possibilities. If we can determine the exact cause of death," Cecily said as she moved over to the door, "that could perhaps help us. In the meantime, I need to find out what it is that connects these three men." And Ian, she added silently.

"Ye know, lassie, I shall have to report my findings to Inspector Cranshaw?"

Cecily nodded. "Yes, I understand that. But I would be most obliged if you could see your way clear to informing me first."

"I can do that." He narrowed his eyes as he looked at her. "If it turns out that you are right about the poison, it will certainly clear Madeline."

"Exactly." Cecily smiled. "Good day, Doctor." Though what it would do for Ian, she thought, her smile fading as she stepped out into the street, that remained to be seen.

The first place she intended to visit was Dolly's Tea Shop. Judging by the faint rumbling in her stomach, it must be very close to midday. A hot sausage roll or Cornish pastie with a cup of tea would go down very well.

She walked briskly along the pavement, pausing now and again to peer into the shop windows in the High Street. A white fur muff caught her eye, and she gazed longingly at it, knowing it was beyond her means. One day, perhaps, when all the hotel bills were caught up. Though goodness knows when that would be.

The pale sun gave little warmth from the hazy sky, and a chill sea breeze stirred the last of the dead leaves lying in the gutter.

In spite of her heavy cloak, Cecily felt quite cold by the time she arrived at the tea shop. The walk and the crisp, fresh air had put color in her cheeks and sharpened her appetite. She was looking forward to her meal with a great deal of pleasure.

The striped awning flapped in a sudden gust of wind as Cecily pushed open the door of the tea shop, to the tune of the jangling bell.

The place buzzed with chatter and quiet laughter, and for a moment she thought she might not have a seat. Then Louise appeared, looking hot and flustered. "Oh, Mrs. Sinclair. How nice to see you again. Do please come this way. The small table in the corner has not been taken as yet."

Cecily edged her way across the crowded room, exchanging smiles and nods with the rest of the clientele seated at the round tables.

"I should like a word with Dolly when she has a spare moment," Cecily said after giving her order.

Louise looked even more agitated. "Oh, I'm afraid Mrs. Matthews isn't here. She has some errands to run, and since the worst of the rush is over, she decided to take advantage of the lull and get her shopping done."

"Oh," Cecily said, disappointed. "Then I shall just have to catch her later. Perhaps she'll be back before I leave."

Louise smiled and nodded. "Perhaps." She hurried off to the kitchen to get the order, while Cecily sat back and loosened her cape. In the time that it took Louise to return with her sausage roll and tea, several of the customers left the tearoom, having finished their lunch.

Cecily waited while Louise poured the first cup for her, then set the teapot down on its stand. "I suppose everyone has heard about the death of the third man last night," Cecily said as Louise turned to leave.

The assistant shot her a nervous glance. "Oh, yes, ma'am. Everyone is talking about it. Though it doesn't seem to have disturbed anyone's appetite. At least not here."

"So I noticed." Cecily smiled. "Dolly must be most gratified about that."

"I'm sure she is, ma'am."

Cecily picked up her spoon and began lazily stirring her tea. "I understand the poor man was here yesterday afternoon."

Louise looked as if she really didn't want to talk about it. "I believe he was, yes, ma'am."

"Did you happen to see him?"

"No, ma'am. I didn't. As I said, we have been busy. I don't remember seeing him at all. Mrs. Matthews spoke to him."

Cecily looked up and was struck by the intent look on Louise's face. Not wishing to explain her unwarranted interest in the dead man, Cecily sought to change the subject.

Her eye fell on the assistant's hand, and the oval-shaped opal she wore. Though it seemed out of place for such a flamboyant piece of jewelry, the stone was quite beautiful, and Cecily said sincerely, "That really is a most unusual ring. May I look at it?"

Obviously pleased, Louise held out her hand for inspection. "It was a gift from my husband," she explained. "He actually dug up the opal himself in Australia, and had it mounted there."

"Really?" Cecily murmured, admiring the vivid colors flashing in the large stone. "Was he a geologist?"

"Oh, no, ma'am. Roger was a medical scientist. He was quite brilliant, really. He traveled all over the world to work on his research projects."

"How interesting." Cecily smiled vaguely up at the woman. She was remembering something Phoebe had told her earlier in the week.

Her husband was a scientist. There's something very mysterious about his death. He was in Central America, working on a science project, and was infected with this strange disease. No one seemed to know what it was.

"Pardon me?" Cecily said, suddenly aware that Louise had said something she hadn't heard.

"I asked if that would be all, ma'am."

Conscious of the other woman's hard, curious stare,

Cecily pulled her scattered thoughts together. "Yes, thank you, Louise. That will be all."

It had to be coincidence, Cecily thought, munching her way through her sausage roll without tasting one bite. Just because Louise's husband died in Central America did not mean the woman was going around killing people with poisoned darts. The idea was quite ludicrous.

She picked up her cup, then put it down again, spilling some of the tea over the side. She didn't notice. She was too busy considering another thought that had struck her. Louise Atkins had arrived in Badgers End shortly before the first man died. Another coincidence?

Anxious to leave now, Cecily drained her cup and beckoned to Louise for her bill.

"I trust everything was satisfactory?" Louise asked as Cecily dug in her handbag for her coin purse.

"Wonderful, as always." Hastily she thrust some money at Louise. "Here, you may keep whatever is left over. Tell Dolly I was sorry to have missed her."

"Oh, thank you. Mrs. Sinclair. Most kind of you, I'm sure. Dolly will be here tomorrow. It's my day off, so she is certain to be here."

"Oh, well, perhaps I shall see her then." Gathering her cape around her, Cecily headed with unseemly haste for the door. This was something she needed to discuss with Baxter. Maybe then she could make some sense out of it.

Wishing she had ordered Samuel to collect her from the tearoom, Cecily set out at a brisk pace for the hotel.

She found Baxter in his office when she arrived back. She felt quite warmed by the fast walk and more than a little out of breath. Baxter looked alarmed when she burst in without knocking as she usually did.

"Is something wrong, madam?" he asked, pulling out a chair for her to sit on.

"No . . . yes . . . I really don't know." She allowed him to take the cape from her shoulders and fanned her face with her gloved hand.

"Can I get you something? A cup of tea? Brandy?"

She heaved in her breath and let it out slowly. "A cigar?" she said hopefully.

Baxter's eyebrows shot up predictably. "Really, madam—"

"Oh, do come on, Bax. I haven't had one in simply ages, and I fine I have a very great need to relax. A cigar will help me to do that admirably."

His face stiff with disapproval, Baxter pulled the package from his pocket and handed it to her. Striking a match with an expert flick of his wrist, he held the flame to the end of her cigar, and she drew in the fragrant smoke.

"Ah . . . that is wonderful. I feel better already."

"I shall remind you of that when you are lying on your bed with a hacking cough."

She gave him a mischievous look. "Why, Baxter, I should certainly hope that if I am lying on my bed, you will not be so indiscreet as to stand there and chastise me."

His cheeks flamed. "Of course not, madam."

For once she received little pleasure from her teasing. She had far too much on her mind. "I suppose you have heard that the police are now questioning Ian?"

"Yes, madam. Mrs. Chubb informed me of the fact shortly after I returned this afternoon."

"I suppose it was inevitable. Though Ian insisted he had no idea why Mr. Sparks should be asking for him."

"I am not altogether certain we can believe every word spoken by that young man," Baxter said stiffly. "I have a strong suspicion that he was not entirely truthful about his reasons for leaving the city."

"I'm afraid you might be right." She told him what Gertie had said about the smuggling. "However," she concluded, "I am inclined to believe he is telling the truth about everything else."

"I shall have to have a word with that young man," Baxter said darkly. "He'll be doing no more smuggling, I can promise you."

Cecily took another puff at the cigar. "In any case, I have some information that I think you will find interesting." She then proceeded to tell Baxter about her morning activities.

His face got darker and darker as she recounted her conversation with the doctor and her subsequent visit to the tea shop.

"I really must implore you, madam," he said when she finally paused for breath, "it could be most dangerous for you to conduct this investigation without proper escort. I must insist that in future you inform me of your intentions, so that I might accompany you."

"You weren't here, Baxter, or I certainly would have," Cecily said mildly. "But what do you think of my discoveries? Do you not think there could be a possibility that Louise Atkins is involved in some way with the murders?"

Baxter rocked back and forth on his heels, running his palm over his hair. "I really don't know what to think, madam. I'm inclined to think it's merely a coincidence. I haven't made the acquaintance of Mrs. Atkins, but by all accounts she seems a most unlikely suspect. What could a woman like that possibly have to do with the men who died? Or Ian, for that matter?"

"That," Cecily said quietly, "is exactly what I intend to find out at the earliest opportunity."

Gertie had her back to the kitchen door, her arms plunged to the elbows in hot steaming water as she bent over the sink. Lifting a soapy dish from the water, she watched the frothy bubbles run down the side.

Still no sign of the curse. And now with Ian in trouble with the law, she could really be lumbered. There she was, stuck with a bun in the oven, and no husband. Ruin her bloody life it would. Who would look at her sideways now, once she had a nipper?

She should never have believed Ian when he told her it was all right. Don't worry, he'd said. What they were doing couldn't possibly get her pregnant, he'd said. Fat lot he knew. She knew it was wrong, but it had felt so good, and with all those sweet words he was whispering in her ear, no wonder she got carried away.

She dipped the plate back into the water, wondering if it

would be possible to get married to him while he was in prison. Blimey, she thought, what a bleeding choice. Either stuck with a baby and no husband, or married to a bloody convict. Good job her old man wasn't around. He'd have her hung, drawn, and quartered, that he would.

The door opened behind her, and she lifted the plate again, shaking the soap from the rim. She was about to stand it on the draining board when a familiar voice said softly, "Hallo, me old love, how's me best girl doing, then?"

With a loud splash the plate fell back in the water, and Gertie spun around. "Ian! Cor blimey, you gave me a start."

He caught her around the waist and hugged her tight. "Got sprung I did, didn't I. Told you there was nothing to worry about."

Blinking back threatening tears, Gertie grinned up at him. "I'm glad to see you, Ian Rossiter, even if you do give me bloody heart attacks."

The door opened again before he could answer, and he stepped smartly away from her.

Cecily looked relieved as she walked into the kitchen. "Ian, I'm so glad to see you. I saw you arrive from my window. I hope you managed to satisfy the police?"

"For the time being, mum. I'll be glad when they find the one what's doing all this, though. Makes me nervous, police stations do. For a bit there I was afraid they was going to lock me up."

Cecily nodded. "I'm sure it must have been upsetting. Did you see Madeline while you were there?"

"Yes, mum, I did. They let her go, too. They took her back to her cottage before they dropped me off. Said they didn't have enough evidence to hold either of us."

"I'm glad to hear that," Cecily said.

"So am I, mum," Gertie said fervently. "I was really, really worried, I was."

"Yes, well, we all were." Cecily sighed. "But it's not over yet, by any means, I'm afraid. Until they find the person responsible for these dreadful murders, both you and Madeline will be under suspicion."

"I know, mum," Ian said gloomily. "They more or less told us that. Things don't look very good for me, I can tell you, what with that detective looking for me. Though no one seems to know why he wanted to see me."

Cecily looked at him in surprise. "Detective? What detective?"

"Oh, you don't know about that, do you?" Ian shoved his hands in his pockets and sent a quick glance over at Gertie. "The last bloke what died, Ted Sparks? He wasn't a reporter at all. He was a private detective working on a case, from what the police can make out. Though they can't figure out what. They're working on it in London now."

CHAPTER
❋17❋

Intrigued by this news, Cecily said urgently, "Think, Ian. You are positive you can't think of a single reason why a London detective should be looking for you?"

Ian looked down at his feet and shuffled from side to side. "No, mum. Can't think of a single reason."

"And you are positive there is no possible connection between you and the first two men who died? Is it possible the detective wanted to ask you about them? Something you might have known about them that could be useful to him?"

Ian frowned. "Can't think of anything, mum. Except that me and Bickley and Donaldson all looked a bit alike. Used to call us the terrible triplets, they did. I never saw it, but some people said we looked like brothers. I think it was just because we all worked together. 'Course, we did all have dark hair and dark eyes, like, and we had the same kind of bodies, not like those big bruisers with all the muscles."

"I like your body," Gertie said stoutly. She then turned a bright shade of red and hastily went back to washing the dishes with a great deal of splashing.

Even Ian looked uncomfortable until Cecily smiled. "But you say you never associated with the men after work?" she asked.

"No, mum, never. Like I said, we was on different sides of the fence."

Sending a look of apology at Gertie, Cecily said quietly, "They weren't involved in the smuggling with you and Mr. Scroggins?"

Ian's face registered shock. He shot a startled look at Gertie, who stared back at him in helpless abjection. "Strewth, Gertie," he muttered.

"It wasn't Gertie's fault," Cecily said. "I made her tell me. She was extremely upset and worried about you, and it was obvious she was keeping something from us. I insisted that she tell me what it was."

"That's the truth, Ian," Gertie said miserably. "Honest."

Ian shrugged. "Well, I'm not doing it anymore, am I. Haven't been out with Dick since I got the job at the lighthouse. None of the blokes on the project know about the smuggling. I'd stake me life on it. Dick won't have nothing to do with any of 'em."

"And what about Louise Atkins?" Cecily asked, watching Ian's face carefully. "Did you know her before she came to Badgers End?"

Ian's eyes widened in astonishment. "The new woman at Dolly's? Never saw her before in me life. What's she got to do with all this?"

"Probably nothing," Cecily said, satisfied with his reaction. "Except for one thing. The three men who died all came down to Badgers End recently from London. So did Louise Atkins."

Ian shook his head. "Yeah, so they did. But what's that got to do with me? I've been down here a year nearly."

"So you have, Ian, so you have." Cecily turned to go, then

paused at the door to look back at him. "But you were living in London before then, were you not?"

Ian nodded. "Yes, mum. All me life."

"That's what makes me think," Cecily said as she stepped into the hall, "that whatever the connection is, it began in London."

She left Ian standing still, staring after her.

A little while later, Cecily came across Baxter. He stood by the French doors in the ballroom, deep in conversation with John Thimble, the gardener. As she approached them, Baxter cleared his throat loudly, and John abruptly cut off whatever he was saying.

Cecily had the distinct feeling that they didn't wish her to know the subject of their discussion, but she had too much on her mind to worry much about it.

The gardener touched a forelock of his white hair, then, mumbling that he had to get back to work, ambled through the glass doors and closed them behind him.

"I want to talk to you," Cecily said, deciding the empty ballroom was as good a place as any in which to hold a conversation. "Ian has returned from the police station."

Baxter nodded. "And Miss Pengrath?"

"Madeline is home also."

"I'm sure that must be a great relief for you, madam."

"It is, Baxter, indeed it is. But Ian had something very interesting to tell me. The third man who died, Ted Sparks, wasn't a reporter at all. He was a London detective working on a case. Though Ian insists he has no idea why a detective should be looking for him. What do you think about that, Baxter?"

She looked up at him, disturbed by his grave expression. "I think, madam, that it's likely the detective was investigating the death of the two men. Undoubtedly that was the reason he was killed."

"Yes, I thought you might come to that conclusion."

"If I am right, that would mean that you could be in considerable danger yourself."

"I realize that, Bax, but I've come too far with this to give it up now. I can hardly go to the inspector with everything I know."

"As I've said before, madam, it would have been better if you had let things alone."

"Piffle. The police would never have worked out the dart thing. It was only by chance that Colonel Fortescue mentioned it to me."

"You don't know yet if that theory is correct."

Cecily smiled up at him. "It's the only thing that makes sense, Baxter. Mark my words, Dr. McDuff will find a puncture wound in the body of Ted Sparks, or my name is not Cecily Sinclair."

The following morning brought fresh rain and a capricious breeze that whipped Cecily's skirt around her ankles as she made her way down the hotel steps to the trap. Sniffing the salty air, she waited while Samuel raised the hood, then climbed in beneath it.

"Dr. McDuff's surgery first, please," she told Samuel. "I shan't be but a minute there, then I need you to take me to Dolly's Tea Shop."

"Yes, ma'am," Samuel said, touching his cap. He flicked his whip, and they were off.

The windswept streets looked so forlorn in the rain, Cecily thought as they rounded the curve to the High Street. How much nicer the village looked when it basked under a warm summer sun.

The trap jogged past St. Bartholomew's, the gray walls of the church looking somber beneath the shade of the chestnut trees. A sharp pang of nostalgia caught Cecily unawares, and she turned her thoughts quickly to the task at hand.

Everything depended on the doctor's findings, of course, but if she was right, she wanted very much to talk to Dolly about her new assistant.

Cecily could hardly contain her excitement when she arrived at the surgery. Dr. McDuff was with a patient, and she waited in a fever of anxiety until he was free to talk to her. She could tell by his face that he had the news she expected to hear.

"You were right, lassie. It's no wonder I missed it before, especially since I wasn't looking for it. But it was there, just behind his right ear. The murderer knew exactly what to do. The dart hit him from behind."

"I knew it." Feeling very pleased with herself, she said, "I am quite sure the other two men must have died the same way. Does that suggest the poison could be curare?"

"It certainly would appear to be, judging from what information I could find on it. There's only one problem, as far as I can see."

Cecily's smile faded. "And what is that?"

"The puncture wasn't made by a dart like the ones used with a dart board. It was something much lighter, smaller, thinner, just a splinter, I would say."

Cecily caught her breath. "Like a piece of bamboo?"

The doctor peered at her from under his shaggy brows. "Exactly. If you remember, Donaldson died in front of several witnesses, yet no one reported seeing a dart lying on the ground. A tiny splinter of wood would blow away in the wind."

"That's it," Cecily whispered. "Dr. McDuff, I know you have to pass this information on to the inspector, but I would be most grateful if you would not mention my part in it."

"Of course, lassie. You can depend on it."

"Thank you." Cecily rose and gathered up her cape. "I think I shall go to Dolly's and have a nice cup of tea."

The doctor took the cape from her and slipped it around her shoulders. "Be careful, lass. Don't be taking any chances now. This is a nasty business, and I don't want to see you hurt. Leave it to the police. They will work it all out, no doubt."

Ah, Cecily thought as she climbed up into the trap, but will they work out the solution in time? Ian's name was on that list, and she had the dreadful feeling that if she didn't put a stop to the murderer's game, whatever it was, Ian could be the next one to turn blue.

*   *   *

Cecily felt perfectly safe walking into the tea shop later, since Louise had told her it was her day off. The rain had brought a steady influx of customers to the tearoom, and Dolly was rushed off her feet, but eventually she found a few minutes to greet Cecily, who sat at her favorite corner table.

"Come and sit with me for a minute or two," Cecily said, watching all but two of the customers finally leave. "I haven't had a chance to chat with you in such a long time."

Dolly glanced around the room, then nodded. "Don't mind if I do. It feels good to take the weight off me feet for a minute."

She plunked herself down on the chair, overlapping it on both sides. Jamming her elbows on the table, she said cheerfully, "You are looking so much better, Cecily. Good to see you smile again."

"I am feeling much better, thank you." Cecily finished her tea and set down the cup. "I can see that business has improved for you, too."

"Yeah, that lighthouse project has really made a difference. I'm going to miss them all when they go back, as will most of the businesses in town. Especially the George." Dolly looked over her shoulder in case anyone was within earshot. "Not doing so good down there now, though, since that last one copped it. People are afraid to eat down there, so I heard. That's probably why I've been so busy."

Cecily nodded. "Good thing you have Louise to help you out. She seems very efficient."

"My lucky day that was, when she came down here." Dolly leaned forward and dropped her voice. "Tragic for her, though, it was. That poor woman has had more than her share, I can tell you."

Cecily tried to hide her avid interest. "Oh? I'm so sorry to hear that. I understand she lost her husband some years ago."

"Yeah, she did." Dolly licked her lips, prepared to indulge

in her favorite hobby. She considered the day a waste if she didn't exchange at least one piece of juicy gossip.

"She told me all about it, one night after we closed up. Gave her a shot of my gin, I did. 'Cause she seemed so depressed. Must have loosened her tongue."

It was more like Dolly's expert questioning that had loosened the woman's tongue, Cecily thought.

"Anyway," Dolly went on, "Louise's only child lost her husband in all that fighting in Africa. Carrying her first baby, she was. She nearly lost it, so Louise said, and spent weeks in bed. Then what do you think? The poor girl died having the baby. After all that." Dolly shook her head in pity. "Anyway, Louise ends up having to take care of the little girl. Then Louise's husband goes and dies in the tropics. Working on a science project, he was. Caught some terrible disease. Poor Louise, all she had left of her whole family was that granddaughter. Brought her up, she did."

Cecily, listening intently, nodded in sympathy. "It must have been dreadfully difficult for her."

"Oh, it was," Dolly said, "it was. But that's not the end of it. Oh, dear no. Something much worse happened after that."

Cecily waited, knowing that Dolly would finish the story even if the tearoom were burning down.

"Well," Dolly said, settling herself more comfortably on the chair, "this granddaughter, see, she meets a chap and falls in love with him. Only he weren't no good. Got her in the family way, then took off. Poor girl was so miserable and ashamed, she went and killed herself. Left a note, she did. Said she was doing the best thing for everyone." Dolly looked down at the tablecloth and heaved a tremendous sigh. "Weren't the best thing for Louise, of course. Near on broke her heart. She couldn't stand to be around London after that. So she hopped it down here. Trying to forget, she is."

"How awful." Cecily paused, then added carefully, "I wonder what kind of research her husband had been working on? Did she say how he caught the disease?"

Dolly thought for a minute. "No, I don't think so. I remember her saying as how he'd been working on something that puts people to sleep. Like an ana . . . ani . . . oh, you know, that stuff what puts people to sleep when the doctor has to cut you."

"Anesthetic," Cecily said. *When injected into the skin, however, a small dose would slow down the heartbeat and put the victim into a deep sleep.* "Thank you, Dolly. Thank you very much."

"That's it," Cecily excitedly told Baxter later, after summoning him to the library. "The curare. Louise's husband must have brought some back with him at some time. Or maybe it was shipped back with his effects after he died. Whichever it is, there's no doubt now that Louise Atkins is our killer."

"But why?" Baxter said, his brow wrinkling in bewilderment. "What possible reason can she have for killing all those men? And why is she after Ian?"

"That I don't know," Cecily said grimly, "but I have an idea it's something to do with the death of her granddaughter. We have to stop her before she gets to Ian."

"I agree. I will go and see the inspector right away and tell him what you have discovered."

"No, Baxter," Cecily said, fixing him with a determined look. "You will not. In the first place, it is unlikely he will take our word for it. He will want to conduct his own investigation, by which time Louise could realize he is on to her. She would either make every effort to complete her list of victims and kill Ian, or she would make good her escape, in which case Ian would be in danger until she is caught."

"Madam, I—"

"In the second place, the inspector is bound to ask several questions, for which you will not have the right answers. May I remind you that the Pennyfoot's existence could be in peril if we antagonize him too much."

Baxter ran an agitated hand over his hair. "Then, pray tell me, madam, what do you intend to do?"

This was going to be a trifle tricky, Cecily thought, but nonetheless she plunged ahead. "Louise still has her room at the George and Dragon. I intend to search it."

"No! I cannot allow you to—"

"You don't have any choice, Bax."

"I shall simply refuse to help you. I shall go to the police. Against your wishes if I have to, but—"

"You would risk Ian's life? And the closure of the Pennyfoot?"

His mouth opened and shut, while he floundered around for an answer. Finally he muttered, "It would be preferable to losing you, madam."

Her heart gave a tiny flutter. "Why, Baxter, that is the very nicest thing you have ever said to me."

Stretching his neck, he ran his finger around the inside of his collar. "Yes, madam."

"I appreciate your concern, Baxter," Cecily said firmly, "but I intend to search that room. If I can prove that Louise is our murderer and hand her over to the inspector, so to speak, he just might forgive me for my interference. It is her day off, so it would be most dangerous to attempt a search today. I shall be forced to do so, however, if you insist on talking to the police."

Baxter wore an expression of quiet desperation. "I shall respect your wishes, madam."

"Good." Cecily began to relax a little. "Very well. I will conduct the search tomorrow, at midday, when Louise will be occupied at the tearoom. The George and Dragon will be busy with the lunchtime crowd, and no one will notice me slipping in there."

Baxter looked more unhappy by the second, but he murmured a resigned, "Yes, madam."

"What I need you to do, Baxter, is to go in there first and find out which room is Louise's. You have that thingamajig you use to open the hotel rooms—you can unlock the door for me. Then you can come and tell me and keep watch downstairs while I slip up there and search the room. If you watch for me through the window, I will signal when I am finished. If I find what I'm looking for, as I feel certain I shall, we can have Samuel drive us to Wellercombe, where we will present the evidence to the inspector. He can then arrange to have Louise detained before she leaves the tea shop at the end of the day."

"It sounds so very simple," Baxter said miserably. "I wonder why I have this terrible feeling that everything is going to go horribly wrong?"

"Because you worry too much, Bax." Cecily smiled up at him, determined he should not see her apprehension. "You will see, it will all work out perfectly. Trust me."

CHAPTER

❇ 18 ❇

Cecily arose early the next morning, after a restless night. The skies had cleared, allowing the sun to warm the windows and turn the heavy dew on the croquet lawns into a carpet of sparkling crystals.

Gazing out across the gardens, Cecily saw John Thimble making his way down the crazy paving path, pushing a loaded wheelbarrow. In spite of his age, and his slightly stooped shoulders, the gardener was strong and healthy, and Cecily reflected, as she often did, how fortunate it was for the Pennyfoot to have such a reliable staff to take care of it.

Every person on the Pennyfoot staff was important to her, in many ways, and she would fight for their well-being as fiercely as any mother defending her young.

She left the window and crossed the room to her bureau where she kept her thick notebook. In it she had kept notes of each development of the past few days. When the time came to explain things to Inspector Cranshaw, she would have a full record to present to him of every detail in the case.

Another reason she had kept the diary, though it wasn't something she cared to dwell upon, was that if something happened to her, the record would be left to pass on to the police.

Taking up her pen, Cecily dipped it into the inkwell, then shook off the excess drops. She opened a new page and wrote carefully, "Today Baxter and I will go to the George and Dragon to search the room occupied by Louise Atkins. There I hope to find the evidence that will prove her guilty of the murders of three men."

Staring at the lines she'd written, Cecily would have given anything to know the content of the words she would be writing next.

"Hallo, me old love!" Ian said cheerfully as he grabbed Gertie around the waist. "How about making me one of those nice juicy ham sandwiches for lunch, then?"

Gertie, who had been busily slicing bread at the kitchen table, whirled away from him, the bread knife held threateningly in her hand. "Whatcha think I am, then, your bleeding servant? Get your own sandwich, Ian Rossiter, and keep those blinking hands off me, or I'll cut 'em off."

Ian's jovial mood vanished. He'd been bored to death the last two days, he'd missed two nights at the pub, and though Gertie had slipped him a brandy or two it wasn't the same as a dirty big foaming pint in his hand.

"What's the bleeding matter with you?" he demanded, staring at Gertie's flushed cheeks. "You've been as prickly as hell for days. If you've gone off me, for Christ's sake say so, and I can go find meself another bit of stuff who's a bit more lively."

To his utter dismay, Gertie promptly dropped the knife and burst into tears.

"'Ere, 'ere," Ian said, patting her on the shoulder with his fingers. "Don't go on like that, then. Tell me what's up."

"Nothing," Gertie managed to say between sobs.

"Got to be something, me old duck. Is it Mrs. Chubb getting on to you?" He lifted her chin and stared at her tear-stained face with real concern. "You're not ill, are you?"

Gertie snatched her chin away. "No, I'm not ill, you big twerp." She gulped, held her breath for several seconds, then blurted out, "I'm blinking pregnant, that's what."

Stunned, Ian stared at her, trying to make sense of her words. "Pregnant? But you can't be."

"Well, I flipping well am." Her chest heaved, but she managed to control the sob. "I tried everything. Hot baths and gin," she said, making a face. "Bloody awful it was, and I even took one of Madeline's potions, but nothing worked. None of it. I'm blinking pregnant, Ian Rossiter, and you're going to have to take care of me."

He wanted to slap her. Shaking with anger, he gritted his teeth and curled his hands into fists. "Oh, no, I'm bloody not. I got caught like that once before. If you're frigging pregnant, Gertie Brown, then you've been mucking about with someone else. It ain't mine. You ain't going to dump it on me. You can go back to whoever it was and tell him that." He spun around and headed for the door.

"I hate you, Ian Rossiter!" Gertie screamed and picked up the knife.

"Good!" Ian yelled back. "Then you won't want me to marry you, will you. If Mrs. Sinclair wants to know where I am, tell her I'm at the bleeding pub. Drowning me sorrows in beer."

He slammed through the door and let it swing to behind him, muffling Gertie's wailing.

Today was perfect for a walk, and Phoebe had thoroughly enjoyed her stroll along the Esplanade. The mid-autumn air had a definite nip in it, giving her a ravenous appetite. Usually she didn't bother with lunch, preferring her afternoon tea at Dolly's, but there were several more hours to go before then, and she was hungry.

She would stop in at the Pennyfoot, she decided, and see if Cecily would care to join her for lunch at the tearoom. That way she could ride in the trap, saving her the long walk back.

Reaching the steps, she pranced up them, anticipating Cecily's pleasure at her invitation. Inside the foyer she spied Mrs. Chubb, bustling down the stairs with her arms full of curtains.

"Why, Altheda," she said in surprise as the housekeeper arrived at the bottom huffing and puffing, "whatever are you doing? Why aren't the maids doing that?"

Mrs. Chubb's red face peered back at her over the mound of red-and-gold damask.

"It's Ethel's half day off," she said, wheezing a little, "and Gertie isn't feeling too well." She paused to get her breath, then added, "Had to get these down before the chimney sweeps come tomorrow."

"You won't be feeling well yourself if you do too much of that climbing up and down," Phoebe said with a frown. She and Altheda had been friends ever since dear Sedgeley had died, and it had always been Phoebe's contention that the housekeeper was entirely too lenient on her staff.

Mrs. Chubb smiled. "Good for the knees, so I'm told."

"Yes, if you're Gertie's age." Phoebe suddenly remembered why she was there. "Is Cecily in her room? I want to invite her to lunch."

"Oh. Madam left with Mr. Baxter just a few minutes ago. You just missed them."

"Oh?" Phoebe shook her head. "I wonder why I didn't see them on the Esplanade. They must have taken the back road." She frowned at Mrs. Chubb. "She didn't say where she was going, by any chance?"

The housekeeper shook her head. "Not a word."

Phoebe stared suspiciously at her for a moment, wondering if that was indeed the truth, then sighed in resignation. "Ah, well, I shall simply have to eat lunch alone, then. Thank you, Altheda."

She turned to go, then paused as she heard her name

called in a voice that was all too familiar. "Mrs. Carter-Holmes! How fortunate to bump into you like this. Could I please have a word with you?"

Phoebe cast a nervous glance at the bearded face of the artist, who had materialized right in front of her. "Oh, Mr. Rawlins. I'm so sorry, I have an urgent appointment. I was on the point of leaving."

The despicable creature actually had the gall to touch her arm. "I won't keep you more than a moment, I promise, but it is most urgent that I speak to you."

Phoebe looked desperately at Mrs. Chubb, but the housekeeper merely nodded, then hurried across the lobby to the kitchen stairs. Deciding to put an end to the ridiculous situation once and for all, Phoebe said in a voice that barely hid her irritation, "Very well, Mr. Rawlins, but I have only a moment to spare."

The artist rubbed his hands together and gave her a fawning smile that she found quite insincere. "I would like to paint your portrait," he said, fixing his strange, dark eyes on her.

Once more she felt herself being drawn down a long, mysterious corridor. She moistened her lips. "My . . . my portrait?" She considered the request in wonder. Gracious heavens, could the man be serious? What was it Mr. Baxter had called him? Renowned, that was it. Why, this could very well make her famous. This could change her life. This could—

"That's if you have no objection to being painted in the nude," Sidney Rawlins added.

Phoebe's mouth slowly opened and hung there. Her headlong rush down the inviting corridor ceased abruptly as icy cold anger swept over her. Her hand itched to slap his face, but she was loath to make contact with that scraggly beard. Heaven knew what might dwell in it. If only she hadn't left her parasol behind that morning.

She closed her mouth and drew herself up to her full height. She was pleased to see that she almost looked him straight in the eye. "Mr. Rawlins," she said in a cold, deliberate voice, "am I to understand that you expect me to take off my clothes in your presence?"

The artist looked a little apprehensive. "I paint nudes, Mrs. Carter-Holmes. I prefer my models to have buxom figures such as yours. I can assure you it is all perfectly respectable. My paintings hang in some of the best galleries in Bond Street."

Phoebe shuddered. The very thought of strange men ogling her naked body on public display was enough to make dear Sedgely rise from the dead and bring down his wrath upon her head.

"Rest assured, Mr. Rawlins," she said icily, "no one will ever set eyes on my body except the Good Lord above when he chooses to take me."

Raising her hands, she settled her hat more firmly on her head. "If you prefer not to precede me, and wish to remain in good health until that momentous event occurs, I suggest you cast out all notions of luring me into your iniquitous studio, or whatever it is you call the place where you do your evil work. Good day to you, sir."

She spun herself around and marched to the door. To her dismay, the dreadful creature followed her, begging her to reconsider. The unmitigated gall of the man appalled her.

As she approached the door she saw Ian Rossiter out of the corner of her eye, rushing ahead of her. Anxious now for help from any quarter, Phoebe bounced forward and took the startled young man by the arm.

"Oh, there you are, Ian. I have been waiting for you. Let us please hurry, or we shall be late."

She practically dragged him out of the door, breathing a sigh of relief when it closed behind her. "Thank you, Ian," she said breathlessly, enjoying the feel of the cool fresh sea air on her face. "I was being pursued by that horrid creature. I just couldn't get rid of him."

"My pleasure, ma'am," Ian said, pulling his cap onto his head. "I'm glad I could oblige."

Phoebe sent a nervous glance back at the door. "Where are you going, Ian?"

"To the George, ma'am. I'm going to have a bit of lunch there."

"Is Samuel taking you?"

Ian shook his head. "He's taken Mrs. Sinclair somewhere. I'm going to take the spare trap myself."

"Wonderful," Phoebe said, breathing easier. "I wonder if you'd mind dropping me off at Dolly's? I'm so afraid that if I walk there, that horrible man will follow me."

Ian gave her a quick grin. "Come with me, Mrs. C-H. I'll see you're all right."

Phoebe smiled her thanks. Such a nice young man. She followed him down the steps and around to the stables at the back.

Bowling along the Esplanade at a fast clip, she felt so much better. It was very pleasant to have the trap to herself. Reminded her of the old days, when dear Sedgely was alive. She sighed. What a shame he had to die like that.

She'd warned him no end of times about leaping over hedges on the back of a huge brute of a horse, chasing a poor defenseless little fox. She had never approved of the ghastly practice, found it quite barbaric, in fact. She always had a notion that dear Sedgely would pay for his misdeeds someday.

Phoebe watched a sea gull glide low across the white-edged waves, then pounce into the water after a hapless fish. Life could be so cruel at times. So very cruel. She had been left to bring up poor Algie alone. He had suffered from the experience.

Not that she believed or even understood all the whispers that went on in the back of the church. Algie was a wonderful vicar, and it wasn't his fault he was too nervous to take any interest in a woman.

Maybe she had been a little protective of him, Phoebe reflected as she leaned back in the bouncing trap, but at least he hadn't turned out like that lascivious creature leering over women's naked bodies.

The chestnut trotted along the High Street with a clatter of hooves, then slowed to a stop in front of Dolly's Tea

Shop. Phoebe waited for Ian to help her dismount. "I am most obliged," she told him, nodding and smiling. "I shall be sure to tell Cecily how kind you have been."

Ian touched his cap. "Enjoy your lunch, Mrs. C-H."

"Thank you, Ian," Phoebe said graciously. "I certainly intend to."

She turned, surprised to see Louise standing in the doorway with the door held open for her. "Oh, my, this is service," Phoebe remarked as she stepped into the fragrant warmth of the tearoom.

"I saw you arrive, ma'am," Louise said with a smile.

"Ah, yes, it isn't often I have the luxury of arriving in a carriage." Phoebe followed the stout woman to an empty table. "Mr. Rossiter was kind enough to drop me off on his way to the George and Dragon. Otherwise it would have taken me a great deal longer to get here."

She seated herself on the chair that Louise had pulled out for her. "Now, I am absolutely starving. I think I shall have one of those delicious Cornish pasties and a nice pot of tea to go with it. Oh, and a Devonshire cream bun, if Dolly has made some today?"

"Yes, ma'am. I'll bring it right away."

Phoebe sat back in contentment. It was really very nice to be treated with such regard by a well-refined lady such as Louise Atkins. How sad that a woman of her class should be forced to work in a tearoom, even if it was a respectable establishment. Such a comedown. Thank heavens she didn't have to resort to such drudgery.

Phoebe looked around at the cozy tables with their white linen cloths, and the silver candlesticks that stood in the center of each one. Bright chintz curtains hung at the windows, and several small paintings of village scenes hung on the walls.

If she were forced to work for a living, Phoebe decided, there were a lot worse places to do so than Dolly's Tea Shop. Her eye fell on the pendulum clock that sat on the mantelpiece above the fireplace. Goodness, it was almost one o'clock. No wonder she was hungry.

She cast a glance over at the doorway, through which she

had expected Louise to appear any minute. Whatever was taking the woman so long?

As if in answer to her question, Dolly popped her head into the room, which was now half-empty. Speaking to no one in particular, Dolly called out, "Has anyone seen Louise?"

The remaining customers looked at each other and shook their heads.

"She went to get my order," Phoebe said helpfully. "A Cornish pastie, tea, and a Devonshire cream bun."

Dolly frowned. "That's strange, I can't find her. She seems to have disappeared. Wherever could she be?"

"Well done, Baxter," Cecily said when Baxter gave her the number of Louise's room and informed her he'd unlocked it. "Now all you have to do is keep an eye on everyone in the bar while I sneak up the back stairs."

They were standing some distance from the George and Dragon, having left the trap hidden down a small lane around the bend in the road.

"I do not like this, madam. I do wish you would allow me to search the room—"

"We don't have time to argue," Cecily said firmly. "It must be very close to one o'clock. We must take advantage of the lunch hour, so that Mr. Scroggins will be too busy to see me go into Louise's room. You know very well I cannot be in the bar watching everyone while you search the room. It has to be this way, Baxter."

"I still think it would be a good idea to simply ask Scroggins to let us search the room."

Cecily sighed. "And what if Mr. Scroggins is involved in this in some way? It is much too dangerous to assume anything, Baxter. Now please hurry, while we still have time to do this without being detected."

Baxter looked down at her, his face creased in concern. "Very well. But I have to tell you, I still have this feeling that we are making a very grave mistake."

Cecily didn't have too good a feeling about what they

were doing, either, but she wasn't about to tell Baxter that. "Don't worry," she told him as they walked toward the George and Dragon, "I will be in and out of there as fast as I can. There is absolutely nothing to worry about."

She found herself wishing she could be sure of that as she waited behind a large oak tree for an opportunity to slip through the back door unseen.

"All clear," Baxter said quietly, as two villagers entered the saloon door. "Try not to take too long—and please, madam, take care."

Cecily nodded. "You also. I will signal from here as soon as I am finished. Watch for me at the window." She waited for his brief nod, then, her heart pounding, she hurried across the grass to the back door.

CHAPTER

❊19❊

Gertie stood at the door of Mrs. Parmentier's room, waiting for the widow to answer her polite tap. Gertie was not in a very good mood. In fact, Gertie was filled with fear and rage. Ian had done the unthinkable. He had denied the baby was his.

How could he do such a thing to her? She'd trusted him. He was the only bloke she'd ever let get near her. Near enough to cause the damage, that was. And to accuse her of doing it with someone else was bloody well disgusting, that's what it was.

Her hands holding the loaded tray trembled. What was she going to do now? How was she going to manage on her own with a nipper to feed and clothe? She could barely afford to clothe herself. And who was going to give her a job anyway? She could hardly carry the thing around on her hip while she did her work. This wasn't bleeding Africa, for Gawd's sake.

The door opened abruptly, making her jump.

Gertie had been prepared for the faceless head behind the thick black veil. She was not prepared for the shiny, round apparition that appeared in the doorway.

Short dark hair hung straight and limp, and one side of the face puckered like crumpled paper, and it glowed with an odd purplish red stain. Two bright blue eyes stared at her, and the mouth was drawn back in a lopsided grin.

Thoroughly unnerved, Gertie let out a shrill scream and dropped the tray. The resounding crash that echoed down the long hallway made things worse. Much worse, she discovered when she looked down and saw all the smashed china, and Michel's famed bouillabaisse all over the carpet.

It was all too much. Gertie covered her face with her apron and howled.

She felt a hand on her arm and a gentle tug, but she was too distraught to resist. The soft hands pushed her down on a chair, while she let it all out in great tearing sobs that shook her entire body.

"Here," Mrs. Parmentier's husky voice said, "take these, you'll feel better."

Gertie held back the next sob and peeked over her apron. She looked at the two small white tablets lying in the large palm in front of her and shook her head.

"They are called aspirin," the widow said. "They are harmless, I promise you. Look, if I swallow one, will you take the other? It will help make you feel better."

Gertie had never heard of aspirin. All she'd ever taken for medicine was Mrs. Chubb's powders.

A glass of clear liquid appeared in Mrs. Parmentier's other hand. "Look," she said, "I'm swallowing one of the aspirin."

Gertie made herself look up at the dreadful face. It didn't seem nearly so frightening now. Ugly, but not frightening. She watched while the widow swallowed the tablet. With a good deal of uncertainty, Gertie took the other one in her shaking fingers.

"Put it on the back of your tongue," Mrs. Parmentier said, "and swallow the water. It will slide down."

Gertie did what she was told. It wasn't a pleasant feeling, but she got it down. Then, without thinking, she said in alarm, "It won't hurt the baby, will it?"

Mrs. Parmentier smiled her lopsided smile. "No, it won't hurt the baby." She sat down on a chair opposite Gertie and looked at her. "Now, why don't you tell me all about it."

Gertie looked into those kind blue eyes, full of sympathy and tenderness, and before she knew it, she was spilling it all out. How she and Ian had done it, and now she was pregnant, and with all the trouble about the murders, and then Ian lying that the baby was his, and how she didn't know what she was going to do.

Mrs. Parmentier nodded throughout it all, then asked a lot of questions that made Gertie blush, but somehow she answered them anyway, without even meaning to. Then Mrs. Parmentier smiled cockeyed at her again.

"My dear," she said softly, "I doubt very much if you are pregnant. From what you've told me, your young man was telling the truth. In order for you to have a baby, he'd have to do much more than he did."

Gertie looked at her in astonishment. "Go on?"

"I have a book I'll be happy to give to you," the widow said. "It will explain everything better than I can. But there's something I want to try. I think I might be able to help you."

She pulled at the chain around her neck and withdrew from her blouse a beautiful yellow stone, set in gold. "I want you to look at this pendant and keep your eyes on it. Just try to relax. I'm going to count down from ten and I want you to watch the pendant."

Gertie stared at the amber stone swinging back and forth in the widow's fingers. She listened to the soft voice counting backward, and suddenly felt very sleepy . . .

Baxter stood in the public bar, having positioned himself so that he had a clear view through the window to the street beyond. If he tilted forward, he could just see the thick oak tree, from where Cecily had arranged to give her signal.

He'd ordered a half-pint of ale, but was too worried to enjoy it. He would gladly leave it on the counter if it meant that Cecily had finished her precarious task and was beckoning to him from the oak tree.

Dick Scroggins, his face flushed and glowing, called out as Baxter looked out the window again. "Hey, mate, haven't seen you down here lately. Good to see you. I could do with some more customers. Been a bit sparse lately."

Baxter smiled and lifted his beer in answer. The pub certainly seemed a lot quieter than he'd noticed before. Usually thirty or forty men crowded into the snug little room, making movement impossible unless one shoved one's way through a thick mass of bodies. Today, however, no more than a dozen men stood drinking at the counter.

Baxter put his beer down, turning his head as he heard the bar door swing open. At least there was one more customer for Scroggins. The more the merrier. Less chance of Cecily being spotted on her way out, with all the noise and confusion that went on when the bar was crowded.

Then he twisted his head back quickly in dismay. To his intense discomfort, the newcomer was someone he knew.

"Why, Mr. Baxter," Ian said behind him. "I'm surprised to see you down here. I didn't know you patronized the George."

Baxter placed a slight smile on his face and looked at him. "Upon occasion I do, Ian."

"Really? So what's the occasion? Maybe I can help you celebrate." Ian held up his hand to catch Dick's attention. "Pint of wallop, me old fruit, if you please."

"Coming up," Dick called out, then stuck a glass under the barrel tap and tugged down on the handle.

"I was simply in need of a change of air," Baxter said, lifting his mug.

"Picked a right place here, then, didn't you," Ian said, nodding at the thick, smelly haze of smoke that filled the room. "Done better to have gone for a walk on the beach."

Baxter leaned forward to take a look out the window. As he did so, he was nudged aside by a thickset man Baxter didn't recognize. The man ordered a beer in a belligerent tone, and Ian said out of the corner of his mouth, "One of them cocky bastards from London."

Dick snarled an answer back and took his time in reaching for a mug.

"If you don't want me frigging business," the man said, leaning his pudgy elbows on the counter, "I can bleeding well get me beer somewhere else."

The rest of the men had stopped talking and watched the proceedings with great interest.

Baxter got a nasty feeling in the pit of his stomach.

"Why don't you do that, mucker?" Dick said, tipping the beer out of the glass into the drain. "Go back to bleeding London where you belong. And take the rest of the yobs with you. Bloody good riddance."

"We'll go when we're good and ready. And I wouldn't be so bleeding anxious to get rid of us if I were you. You won't get your frigging lighthouse built if you don't watch it."

Dick, who had obviously been imbibing for some time, leaned across the counter and stuck his nose in the laborer's face. "I don't want the bleeding lighthouse built, mate. And if you build it up again, I'll be back to knock it down again, won't I."

For a moment the Londoner stared at Dick in astonishment, then with a howl of rage grabbed the publican by his collar and dragged him over the counter, yelling, "We lost our bleeding wages because of you, you bastard!"

Before Baxter could move, a dozen men surged up to the two combatants and joined in the fracas, pinning Baxter into the corner. He lunged forward, only to meet a solid fist to the nose.

The last thing he remembered was seeing a dozen circles of light, all rotating around each other through the smoky haze.

"It weren't half queer, the way she did it," Gertie told Mrs. Chubb who, much to her delight, was hanging on her every word. "Just sort of waved this jewel around, she did, and I fell fast asleep. When I woke up, she said everything would be all right in a day or two."

Mrs. Chubb looked impressed. "How did she do that, then?"

Gertie polished the fork in her hand with renewed vigor. It amazed her how much better she felt. Like a new person. "She used to be a doctor," she told Mrs. Chubb, "the kind what puts people to sleep, then tells their mind what to do. She said as how I wasn't pregnant, but because I was worried about it, that's what was holding everything up. She said that now the worry was gone and I was relaxed, it will all sort itself out again."

Mrs. Chubb nodded. "Marvelous. Shame about her face, though."

"Yeah." Gertie stopped polishing and stared into space. "She said she'd always been upset about her looks, 'cos she's so big and clumsy. Her parents were German, she said, and all her family's like that. She said she always thought men liked their women tiny and helpless, like."

She glanced down at her own generous curves. "Gawd help me, then, that's all I can say."

"Not all men like small women, otherwise the big ones would never get married."

"Yeah, well, she knows that now. But she said that's why she never got married, 'cos she never gave a bloke a chance to get to know her."

Mrs. Chubb gave a start of surprise. "Then she's not a widow?"

"Nah." Gertie shook her head. "See, when her house caught fire and she got her face burnt, it left her looking so ugly, she said no man would ever look at her after that. So she pretended to everyone she was a widow and covered herself with that veil."

She sighed and put down the fork. "Funny thing is, when you get used to it you don't notice it so much. I mean, it isn't that bad. But that's why she went out at night—it was the only time she would walk along the beach without her veil.

Said she loved to feel the wind on her face, but didn't want people staring at her."

"What a shame." Mrs. Chubb counted out a pile of serviettes. "There are some men out there who don't care what a woman looks like. It's what she's like inside that counts."

"Yeah. Like that Mr. Rawlins."

Mrs. Chubb looked up sharply. "Mr. Rawlins? What's he got to do with anything?"

Gertie smiled. "Well, he's the one what got Mrs. Parmentier to take off her veil. Said she had a beautiful body. Said he wanted to paint it. When she told him she had a terrible scared face, he made her let him look at it." She picked up another fork and smiled at her reflection in it.

"Go on," Mrs. Chubb said, her counting forgotten. "So what happened?"

"Well, when he saw it, he said it wasn't nearly as bad as she made out. That it didn't matter what her face looked like. He could tell she was a loving, caring person, and that's what matters."

Gertie looked up, her eyes sparkling. "She said it made her think, and he gave her the courage to face the world again, even if people did stare at her. She's even going back to being a doctor again. And it's all thanks to Mr. Rawlins."

"Well, that's a turn-up for the books, to be sure. Whoever would have thought it?"

"It just goes to show," Gertie said thoughtfully, "you can't tell what people are really like just by looking at them. Most of the time they're a lot different than what you think."

"You never said a truer word than that, Gertie, my girl."

"Anyway, Mrs. Parmentier seemed quite taken with Mr. Rawlins. Wouldn't it be lovely if he fell in love with her and they lived happy ever after?"

"Go on, you silly goose," Mrs. Chubb said. "Full of romantic notions you are. Better get on with your work before Michel gets back and starts complaining." But she said it with a twinkle in her eyes.

*   *   *

Cecily looked around the neat room, trying to decide where to start. The chest of drawers seemed a likely place, but she was quite sure that if Louise was hiding anything as dangerous as a poisonous drug, she wouldn't casually leave it in a drawer, where anyone could find it.

Not that she would be expecting anyone to be searching her room, of course, Cecily told herself as she crossed to the chest. She had to start somewhere.

She pulled the drawers open one by one, hating what she was doing but acknowledging the necessity of it. The piles of neatly folded underwear slipped through her fingers. Louise Atkins believed in buying the best.

Pure silk and glossy satin, delicate lace-trimmed petticoats and hand-embroidered drawers all shouted of a woman used to wealth and luxury.

Feeling very much like a common intruder, Cecily went on searching through the various drawers without much success. She found nothing out of the ordinary, and obviously she would have to ferret out a more sophisticated hiding place.

Climbing onto her hands and knees, she peered under the bed. Nothing but a few dust balls. Carefully she ran her fingers along the iron frame, hoping to find a container of some sort, and terrified of pricking her finger if she did.

She didn't hear the door open. The first she knew of someone's presence was when a voice asked quietly, "Is this what you are looking for?"

Cecily jerked her head up, then scrambled to her feet, her heart hammering wildly.

Louise stood just inside the doorway, holding a short length of bamboo pipe. She wore a faint smile on her face, but her eyes were cold and calculating. The eyes of a killer.

Cecily sought frantically in her jumbled mind for any reason, no matter how absurd, to explain her presence. She could come up with nothing. She was in a public house, searching under the bed in what had been a locked room. There simply was no explanation for that.

She looked helplessly at Louise, who seemed to be enjoying her predicament. The perception sent chills chasing down Cecily's back.

"It really will be a quick death," Louise said in a conversational tone, "though I can't promise it will be painless. I have already loaded the pipe with enough poison to kill three men. It will do you no good to attempt to avoid the dart. I have excellent aim."

Desperately Cecily tried to make her cold lips move. If she could keep the woman talking long enough, perhaps Baxter would come and investigate. It was possible he had seen Louise arrive and was, at this very moment, rushing up the stairs to her rescue.

Before she could speak, Louise added calmly, "My husband taught me how to use it, as a means of self-defense, since I was living alone in the city so much. I would consider this a case of self-defense, would you not? It should be a simple matter to drag your dead body to the stairs and push it down. They will merely assume that the murderer has struck again, in the halls of the George and Dragon."

She laughed, a dry, hollow sound that frightened Cecily far more than her words had done. The woman was quite insane, her brain turned, no doubt, by so many deaths in her family.

Helplessly Cecily watched as Louise began to lift the pipe slowly to her mouth.

"Don't worry, my dear," Louise said softly. "I have only to hit the skin on any part of your body, and in seconds you will be quite, quite dead."

CHAPTER

✾ 20 ✾

Baxter blinked as he felt strong hands helping him to his feet. He shook his head, his eyes watering at the pain in his nose. Good Lord, he thought, he must have been hit by a train.

The room whizzed around him a couple of times, then slowed, as if he were on a roundabout at the fair.

"Give him a brandy," someone said, and pressed a cold glass into his hand.

He stared down at it, realizing where he was and how he'd come to feel as if he'd been thrown down a cliff. He was in the bar at the George and Dragon. It seemed very quiet. Apparently the fight was over.

Hard on the heels of that thought came another one. *Cecily.* How long had he been out? He threw back his head and emptied the glass into his open mouth. The fiery liquid burned all the way down to his stomach, but it had the desired effect.

His eyes snapped open and, coughing, he spun around to look out of the window. With a rush of relief he saw no sign of Cecily behind the oak tree.

Beside him, Ian said, "Took quite a bashing there, Mr. Baxter, I must say. Hope you're feeling better now?"

Baxter heard the hint of admiration in Ian's voice and smiled thinly. "Yes, thank you. My head is harder than it looks. May I reimburse you for the brandy?"

Ian shook his head. "It was on the house. Dick was sorry about you getting socked."

Baxter looked over at the publican, who looked a little dazed, but otherwise still functioning. "He has a lot more to be sorry about, I'm sure. When the police get word that he was responsible for the damage to the lighthouse project, he'll no doubt have to face charges. He will most likely have to pay for the new equipment."

Ian laughed and laid his finger along on his nose. "Nah, not on your life. All he'll do is hand out a few bottles of France's best cognac, and the lads'll keep quiet about what happened."

Baxter raised his eyebrows, but before he could comment, Ian added with a grin, "Bet the row upset Dolly's new waitress, though. Good job she's moving. She'll be bloody glad to get out of here, I reckon."

Baxter stared at him, hoping he didn't mean what he thought he meant. "Louise Atkins?"

Ian nodded. "Must be her day off. She got back a little while ago. I saw her going past the window when we was all fighting. She must have gone up to her room."

With a muffled oath Baxter slammed his glass down on the counter. "Come with me," he ordered Ian, then headed grimly for the stairs.

"Just tell me one thing," Cecily said, having finally found her voice. "Why would you want to hurt Ian? He doesn't even know you."

Louise gave a short laugh. "Very clever, Mrs. Sinclair. I don't know how you worked that out, but you're right. Ian Rossiter doesn't know me. But I think he might very well have known my granddaughter."

She talked, Cecily thought with a shiver, as though she were holding a normal conversation at some pleasant social event.

"She was abandoned by the father of her unborn child," Louise went on, "and unable to face the shame of it, she threw herself off Westminster Bridge. She landed on a barge below and broke her neck. She died instantly. That man must pay for his sins."

Cecily felt a stab of sympathy, but her eyes remained fixed on the bamboo pipe in the other woman's hand. "But Ian has lived in Badgers End for the past twelve months."

"I understand he travels to the city most weekends, does he not?"

Cecily frowned. "But if you suspect Ian of being the father, why were the other men killed?"

The hand holding the pipe jerked, sending another cold chill down Cecily's back. "That stupid detective. I hired him to find the man who seduced my daughter. All I knew about him from the little my granddaughter had told me was his age, vaguely what he looked like, and that he worked down here on the lighthouse project."

Her best chance, Cecily thought, was to wait until the very last minute, then drop to the floor behind the bed. If, by the grace of God, Louise missed her with the dart, she might possibly have a chance to reach the woman before she could reload the pipe.

That was assuming she had another dart. It was a possibility Cecily couldn't afford to ignore.

"Anyway," Louise went on, "when the fool came back from his investigation, he told me he could get nothing from the men he questioned. The best he could do was to narrow it down to three men. So I decided that all three men must die, in order to be sure that the right one paid for what he did."

Great heavens, Cecily thought. Now she knew the woman was insane. "But why did you—" she began, but Louise cut her off, freezing her blood.

"Enough of this talk. I'm afraid, Mrs. Sinclair, you have asked your last question. It is really a shame that you couldn't keep your nose out of my business. I am so sorry I have to do this."

Cecily tensed as Louise lifted the pipe to her lips, then closing her eyes, she dropped to the floor. As she did so she heard the door handle rattle, a loud thud, and a muffled exclamation.

Without thinking, she raised her head, in time to see Louise staring at her hand that was pinned against the wall in front of her face. Baxter stood in the doorway, his face white as a sheet, looking at Cecily as if he'd never seen a woman before.

"Madam! Are you all right? You weren't hit, were you?"

Too shaken to speak, Cecily shook her head and climbed unsteadily to her feet, her gaze returning to Louise.

She heard Ian mutter, "Bloody hell," but her attention was on the other woman.

Louise made an odd sound, then turned her head with an awkward, stiff movement, her eyes wide and glaring at Cecily with a horrible fiendish light. "You . . ." she said in a strangled voice, then clutched her throat.

"Do something, Bax," Cecily cried, but knew he couldn't. It was much too late to help the stricken woman.

Louise made a gurgling sound and slowly collapsed onto the floor. She thrust out an arm in appeal, her fingers curled like claws. A terrible rattling sound poured from her throat as her body twisted and curled in violent spasms, and her eyes rolled wildly in her head.

Cecily could watch no more. She sank onto the bed and covered her face with her hands until the awful sound had ceased.

"It's over, madam," Baxter said quietly.

He stood next to her, very close but not touching her. She felt a strong urge to seek comfort from him, longed to hold his hand, but knew she could not. "Thank you, Baxter," she whispered. "You saved my life."

He cleared his throat. "I think it was more a matter of fortune, madam. But I am happy to have been of assistance."

For some reason the trite words made her want to weep.

Gertie and Mrs. Chubb sat huddled in front of the roaring oven as Ian gave them the gory details of Louise's last moments.

"Strewth," Gertie whispered when he'd finished, "that must have been bloody awful to watch. Poor madam, she must have felt dreadful."

"She'd have felt a lot more dreadful if Mr. Baxter hadn't rushed in when he did," Ian said with relish. "He slammed the door open, and Mrs. Atkins was standing right there in front of it. Sent her into the wall, it did. Mr. Baxter says she put her hand up against the wall to stop her face from hitting it. The pipe was in her mouth and she puffed the dart right into her blinking hand."

"Serves her bloody well right," Gertie declared, shuddering. "She would have killed madam, and you as well."

Ian gave her a cold look that seemed to cut her in half. "Would have been all right for you if she had, wouldn't it? Then you could have blamed me for what happened to you, and no one would know the difference."

Gertie opened her mouth to protest, but Mrs. Chubb got up noisily from her chair. "Well, I can't sit around here listening to gossip all day," she said, giving Gertie a meaningful look. "Finish what you have to say to Ian, my girl, then get on with those dishes. They'll be twice as hard to wash if the food dries on them."

"Yes, Mrs. Chubb," Gertie said meekly, and watched the housekeeper bustle out of the door.

"I'm going, too," Ian said, making for the door. "The new equipment arrived this afternoon, so I'm back on the job. You won't be seeing me around here for a while."

"Ian," Gertie said as he reached the door, "I'm not pregnant."

He looked back at her. "You was just pretending that you was?"

"No, of course not, you big twerp." She got up from the chair and walked toward him. "I thought I was. But I didn't understand. Mrs. Parmentier told me I couldn't be, she gave me a book and . . ."

She felt her cheeks growing warm but was determined to finish, no matter how blinking awkward she felt. "Well, I know how it happens now. I didn't before. I really thought you'd gone and done it. But I know now you couldn't have, and I've never been with nobody else but you, Ian love, I swear it."

He stared at her, confusion all over his face. "Mrs. Parmentier?"

"It's a long story," Gertie said softly, "but if you come back tonight, I'll tell it to you then. Perhaps I can get the night off so we can go to the bonfire party on the beach."

He looked at her for a moment longer, then gave her his warm, wonderful grin. "All right, me old love, I'll be back tonight, then." Leaning forward, he gave her a loud smack on the cheek, then vanished through the door.

Hugging herself, Gertie smiled and went back to the sink to tackle the dishes.

"I trust everything went well at the police station, madam?" Baxter asked as Cecily sat enjoying one of his cigars at the library table.

"Yes, thank you. I was a little concerned when the inspector wouldn't let you come with me, but I think I handled it all right. I had to leave out the piece about searching the body, of course. I told him I found the list when I searched the room."

Baxter nodded gravely. "That was very clever of you, madam."

He stood with his back to the fireplace in his customary

position, hands behind his back and rocking slightly on his heels.

Cecily blew out a thin stream of smoke. "Yes, I was rather ingenious, if I say so myself. Mind you, there were one or two tricky questions that I couldn't answer, but I managed to change the subject and throw Cranshaw off the track. He was quite angry, of course, about my visit to the George and Dragon to search Louise's room, but he was forced to admit it ended well."

"I expect he gave you a stern warning about repeating such foolhardy escapades in the future?"

"Yes, Baxter, he did. I'm sure you'll be most pleased to hear that."

"I should feel a great deal more comforted if I could be certain you would pay heed to his advice."

She grinned. "Why, Baxter, whatever do you mean? I wouldn't dream of risking my life and limb in such dangerous ventures again."

He gave her a look that said quite clearly he was inclined to disbelieve that statement. He said nothing, however.

"The one thing that had me puzzled at first," Cecily said, adroitly switching to another subject, "was why Louise found it necessary to kill Ted Sparks. The inspector told me that the London police searched his office. According to the detective's notes, he had given up the case. But when Louise decided to take matters into her own hands, Mr. Sparks must have read about the deaths of Mr. Bickley and Mr. Donaldson and put two and two together."

"So he came down to Badgers End to warn Ian?" Baxter said with remarkable intuition.

"I imagine that was his intention, as well as to investigate the case further. Apparently he couldn't find Ian at the boardinghouse and had inquired at Dolly's where he could find him. Louise had seen Mr. Sparks there and followed him to the George and Dragon to stop him from talking to Ian."

"But how did she know you were searching her room?"

"She didn't," Cecily said, stubbing out her cigar. "Ian had

taken Phoebe to the tearoom before going on to the George and Dragon. Phoebe told Louise where Ian was going, and Louise must have decided to take advantage of the opportunity. From what the inspector and I surmise, the dart she carried was for Ian. She must have gone to her room for something first, perhaps to wait until the fight was over, and that's when she found me."

Baxter raised his eyes to the ceiling for a moment, then looked back at her. "You gave me some very anxious moments, madam. When I first opened that door and saw just the top of your head . . ." He shook his head, leaving the sentence unfinished.

Cecily smiled. "How is your nose? Does it still hurt?"

Baxter touched his nose carefully with the tips of his fingers. "I think it will mend. It infuriates me that I was so careless. Had I been better prepared, I could have given a much stronger account of myself."

"I don't doubt that for one second, Bax. And I will tell you, I was never more pleased to see anyone in my life than in that moment when I looked at the door and there you were."

Baxter stretched his chin in the air. "I am just happy that everything turned out so well."

"So am I. Madeline seems to have recovered from the ordeal, though I doubt she will have learned much of a lesson from it."

"There are some people who find it inordinately difficult to pay heed to their reservations."

She looked at him suspiciously, but he stared back at her with an air of sublime innocence.

"Well," she said, "the one regret I have now is that all this excitement has put my schedule entirely out of system. It is November the fifth, and I have done nothing about the fireworks display. I'm quite sure I have ruined the entire year for Colonel Fortescue."

Baxter cleared his throat. "With apologies, madam, but since you were otherwise engaged, I took it upon myself to make some arrangements with John Thimble. If you would care to come with me, you can inspect the display which we set up in the roof garden."

Cecily looked at him in pleased astonishment. "Why, Baxter, how very thoughtful. The guests will be extremely happy that they will not miss out on the festivities, as shall I for not having to tell them it's canceled." She rose to her feet. "I shall be happy to go to the roof garden right now and see for myself."

Baxter, looking uncommonly pleased with himself, opened the door for her.

As she passed under the portrait, she looked up. "There you are, you see, James, he takes very good care of me, as well as the Pennyfoot. You have chosen well."

Baxter stood back to let her pass, murmuring as she did so, "I fear Mr. Sinclair would be most disturbed if he could see how imprudent his wife can be at times."

Cecily paused, leaning back to send another look at the portrait. "Don't listen to him, James," she said. "He can be an intolerable fussbudget."

Smiling, she sailed through the door.